Dearest Father

Franz Kafka

Translated by
Hannah and Richard Stokes

**ONEWORLD
CLASSICS**

ONEWORLD CLASSICS LTD
London House
243-253 Lower Mortlake Road
Richmond
Surrey TW9 2LL
United Kingdom
www.oneworldclassics.com

Dearest Father first published as *Brief an den Vater* in 1953
English Translation © Hannah and Richard Stokes, 2008
First published by Oneworld Classics Limited in 2008
Reprinted 2010
Notes and Introduction © Hannah and Richard Stokes, 2008
Front cover image © Corbis

Printed in Great Britain by CPI Cox & Wyman, Reading, Berkshire

ISBN: 978-1-84749-025-4

Contents

Introduction

Like much of Kafka's work, *Brief an den Vater* (*Dearest Father*) provides interesting insight into the author's attitudes to law and order. Kafka often described his relationship with his father, Hermann Kafka, as a *"Prozess"* ("trial"), and legal terms such as *"Urteil"* ("judgment" or "sentence") and *"Schuld"* ("guilt") feature repeatedly in the letter. When he sent it to his mistress, Milena Jesenská, Kafka himself wrote: *"Und verstehe beim Lesen alle advokatorischen Kniffe, es ist ein Advokatenbrief."** ("As you read it, try to understand all the lawyerly tricks, after all it is a lawyer's letter"). Kafka was interested in systems of social control, and in the *Brief* he criticizes his father as ruler and judge of the family. Kafka finds fault with the inconsistency of Hermann's system: *"Du [musstest] gar nicht konsequent sein und doch nicht aufhörtest Recht zu haben."** ("You did not even have to be at all consistent, and could still never be wrong"). In so doing he usurps the judicial role and gains intellectual supremacy over his father. If his argument appears aggressive, however, we are reminded by its written medium that Kafka was too timid

7

to address his father face to face – in direct confrontation, Hermann would interrupt and throw him off course. Even in writing, Kafka confesses not entirely to have been able to express his argument, which is as inconsistent as the system it attacks. He admits (whether or not in earnest) to deliberately angering his father and at times defends Hermann: "*Du wirktest so auf mich, wie Du wirken musstest,*"* ("Your effect on me was the effect you could not help having"). Kafka's tone changes as often as his standpoint: a sober description of the son's banishment to a distant world of subservience is directly preceded by a comically grotesque depiction of the father digging in his ears with a toothpick and sending scraps of food flying. These oscillations of argument and tone, combined with a highly idiosyncratic approach to punctuation (discussed below), undermine any assertion that the letter is an "*Advokatenbrief*". It lacks the requisite persuasion and reasonableness.

And so the letter presents systems of law and order in a chaotic way. Thomas Anz appears to notice this fusion of order and chaos when he distinguishes between the two thematic levels of the letter. Its surface structure is controlled. Themes are dealt with one by one and include "upbringing, business, Judaism, [Kafka's] existence as a writer, occupation, sexuality and marriage".* In the former three of these sections, Kafka criticizes the examples that his father set:

hypocritically subjecting others to rules that he himself never followed; treating his employees appallingly; and neglecting the religious traditions that were important to his son.* In the latter four sections, Kafka explores his own self-loathing, which stems from his inability to equal his father either by succeeding financially or by founding his own family. Try as he might to impose structure on his thoughts, however, he does not fully confront, analyse or communicate certain underlying issues identified by Anz ("anxiety and guilt, accusations and condemnations, freedom and power, artistry and profession, sexuality").* These unresolved issues dominate much of Kafka's literary output and day-to-day correspondence. They bleed into each of the letter's seven proposed thematic sections, subtly undermining the author's superficial assertion of structure and rationality.

At first glance the letter may appear to document Kafka's exploration of his own insecurities, and his finding their origins in his relationship with his domineering father. As already mentioned, however, the conclusions he draws are not entirely reliable. He wrote the *Brief* in November 1919 at a sanatorium in Schelesen, while recovering from tuberculosis, which had been diagnosed the previous year. At thirty-six, he was just four years away from death. Kafka's illness, coupled with the recent breakdown of his relationship with Julie Wohryzek (his second significant lover), may well have agitated his mind and increased his self-confessed tendency to exaggerate.

It is unclear whether the letter was ever truly intended for the eyes of Hermann Kafka. After writing it by hand, Kafka made a second typed copy (minus the last few pages). He later annotated it in places, with the intention of having it proofread by Milena. Kafka asked his mother to forward one copy to his father – but she could not bring herself to deliver it, and this may have been exactly what the son had hoped for. The *Brief* was part of the bundle of fragments and letters that Kafka entrusted to Max Brod on his death. The instruction was to burn everything; of course, the friend famously published it all, and the whole letter first appeared in 1953.

Kafka's insecurities and motives for writing the letter seem very real. But the work's thematic stylization, its duplication and proofreading, and its failure to reach its addressee are not reminiscent of usual letter-writing practice. Perhaps this is why Brod published the letter with a collection of fictional short stories,* and not with Kafka's autobiographical material. Interestingly, the letter bears many similarities to Kafka's earlier fictional work, *Das Urteil* (1912). This story describes a confrontation between its protagonist Georg Bendemann and his father, triggered when the father reads a letter written by the son. The story begins with the son poised to acquire a wife and enter adulthood, the father ready to die. The father prevents this natural handover of familial power, however, by forbidding Georg to marry (*"Ich fege sie dir von der Seite weg"** ("I'll sweep her away from your side")), and using his last vestige of paternal authority to sentence Georg to death. Some of this occurs in the *Brief an den Vater*. Kafka holds his father in part responsible for his own failure to marry and enter true adulthood. Meanwhile, Bendemann Senior's disapproval of Georg's fiancée – *"weil sie die Röcke so gehoben hat, die widerliche Gans"** ("because she hitched up her skirts, like this, the disgusting cow") – is reminiscent of Hermann's comment about Kafka's fiancée (Felice Bauer) in the *Brief*: *"Sie hat wahrscheinlich irgendeine ausgesuchte Bluse angezogen, wie das die Prager Jüdinnen verstehn"** ("She probably put on some sort of fancy blouse, as only those Prague Jewesses know how"). Like Georg, furthermore, Franz falls to pieces in face-to-face conflict with his father. And so in writing about Georg's death, Kafka was perhaps anticipating his own father's reaction to the real-life *Brief*. He admitted the autobiographical significance of *Das Urteil* in a private diary entry: *"Georg hat so viele Buchstaben wie Franz... Bende aber hat ebenso viele Buchstaben wie Kafka..."** ("Georg has the same number of letters as Franz... Bende has exactly as many letters as Kafka"). Even if the letter's narrative is true, much of it was first rehearsed in fiction.

The letter's ambiguous position between fact and fiction, order and chaos, makes it a fascinating subject for translation. Here it is worth considering two questions: How far can *any* piece of writing be purely factual and objective? And how far should translators seek to impose order on a text whose chaos is integral to its meaning? First, the question of objectivity. No "factual" writing is without an element of fiction. Even if Kafka had intended the letter to be a true representation of events, its composition would have involved some inter-pretation and translation – the author first forming a biased and retrospective view of his childhood, then ordering his thoughts and emotions, and then converting them into words on paper. Much information would have been lost and created in these transformations, and what appears on the page could not be a purely factual reproduction of original events. By confessing to indulge in further creative exaggeration, Kafka is arguably embracing the fictional element of his writing and encouraging the reader to acknowledge his identity as a writer (an identity with which he struggled, according to Anz).* Translators in turn must be aware that, although they attempt to recapture the original text accurately, they will inevitably transform it further. How much transformation is desirable here? This leads to the second question: that of orderliness. The *Brief* contains awkward patterns of syntax and repetition, idiosyncratic use of punctuation and numerous other irregularities. Although Kafka uses only the simplest of words, he arranges them in complex ways to create obscure linguistic effects and produce a text that is often ambiguous. Perhaps these effects are deliberate and intended to put the reader ill at ease. Or perhaps Kafka meant to express himself clearly but was prevented by his illness and emotional instability. Whatever their cause or purpose, the irregularities leave translators in a quandary: should they tidy up Kafka's awkwardness and gloss it for the reader, or rather attempt to preserve it in translation? It is commonly held that a good translation should read smoothly and idiomatically, as if the text were written in English originally. A reader should not expect to have to stumble through a clumsy translation. But where that clumsiness is crucial to the essence of the original, surely it would be insensitive to remove it? Rewriting the *Brief* in refined, consistent or idiomatic English will undermine the awkwardness of Kafka's fevered, fermented German original and do an injustice to its emotional content. In this instance we must therefore break some of the laws of translation, in an attempt to satisfy the demands of the text.

– Hannah and Richard Stokes, 2008

Hannah Stokes read German and French at Emmanuel College, Cambridge. There she studied Kafka's *Brief an den Vater* under the guidance of Dr Michael Minden, to whom she is most grateful. She went on to study law and is now a trainee solicitor. This is her first book.

Richard Stokes is Visiting Professor of Lieder at the Royal Academy of Music in London. He has published a number of books on French, German and Spanish Song, including *The Book of Lieder* – the original texts of over 1000 songs with parallel translations, and an introduction by Ian Bostridge (Faber, 2005).

Dearest Father

Dearest Father,

You asked me recently why I claim to be afraid of you. I did not know, as usual, how to answer, partly for the very reason that I am afraid of you, partly because an explanation of my fear would require more details than I could even begin to make coherent in speech. And if I now try to answer in writing it will still be nowhere near complete, because even in writing my fear and its consequences raise a barrier between us and because the magnitude of material far exceeds my memory and my understanding.

To you the matter always seemed very simple, at least in as far as you spoke about it in front of me and, indiscriminately, in front of many others. To you it seemed like this: you had worked hard your whole life, sacrificed everything for your children, particularly me, as a result I lived "like a lord", had complete freedom to study whatever I wanted, knew where my next meal was coming from and therefore had no reason to worry about anything; for this you asked no gratitude, you know how children show their gratitude, but at least some kind of cooperation, a sign of sympathy; instead I would always hide away from you in my room, buried in books, with crazy friends and eccentric ideas; we never spoke openly, I never came up to you in the synagogue, I never visited you in Franzensbad,* nor otherwise had any sense of family, I never took an interest in the business or your other concerns, I saddled you with the factory and then left you in the lurch, I encouraged Ottla's* obstinacy and while I have never to this day lifted a finger to help you (I never even buy you the occasional theatre ticket), I do all I can for perfect strangers. If you summarize your judgment of me, it is clear that you do not actually reproach me with anything really indecent or malicious (with the exception, perhaps, of my latest marriage plans), but rather with coldness, alienation, ingratitude. And, what is more, you reproach me as if it were my fault, as if I might have been able to arrange everything differently with one simple change of direction, while you are not in the slightest to blame, except perhaps for having been too good to me.

This, your usual analysis, I agree with only in so far as I also believe you to be entirely blameless for our estrangement. But I too am equally and utterly blameless. If I could bring you to acknowledge this, then – although a new life would not be possible, for that we are both much too old – there could yet be a sort of peace, not an end to your unrelenting reproaches, but at least a mitigation of them.

Strangely enough, you seem to have some idea of what I mean. This might have been why you recently said to me, "I have always been fond of you; if, on the outside, I have not treated you as fathers usually treat their children, it is just because I cannot pretend as others can." Now, Father, I have on the whole never doubted your goodness towards me, but this statement I consider wrong. You cannot pretend, that is true, but purely for this reason to claim that other fathers pretend was either sheer indisputable bigotry, or – and this, in my view, is more plausible – a veiled way of saying that something is wrong between us, and that you are partly responsible for it, albeit through no fault of your own. If this is what you really meant, then we are agreed.

I am not saying, of course, that I have become what I am purely under your influence. That would be a very great exaggeration (although I do have a tendency to exaggerate). It is very possible that, had I grown up entirely free of your influence, I still could not have become a person after your own heart. I would probably still have become a weak, anxious, hesitant, restless person, neither Robert Kafka nor Karl Hermann,* yet still very different from what I am today, and we would have been able to get on very well. I would have been happy to have you as a friend, a boss, an uncle, a grandfather, even indeed (though rather more hesitantly) as a father-in-law. It is only as a father that you were too strong for me, particularly since my brothers died young and my sisters did not come along until much later, so I had to endure the initial conflicts all alone, for which I was far too weak.

Compare the two of us: me, to put it very briefly, a Löwy* with a certain Kafka core that is simply not driven by the Kafka will to live, prosper and conquer, but by a Löwy-like force that moves more secretly, more timidly, in a different direction, and which often breaks down completely. You, by contrast, a true Kafka in strength, health, appetite, loudness of voice, eloquence, self-satisfaction, worldly superiority, stamina, presence of mind, understanding of human nature, a certain generosity, of course with all the faults and weaknesses that go with these advantages, into which you are driven by your natural disposition and sometimes your hot temper. Perhaps you are not wholly a Kafka in your general worldly outlook, in as far as I can compare you with Uncles Philipp, Ludwig and Heinrich.* That is odd, and here the picture is no clearer. However, they were all cheerier, fresher, more casual, more relaxed, less strict than you. (In this respect, incidentally, I have inherited much from you and have taken far too great a care of that inheritance, admittedly without having the necessary counter-qualities that you do.) Yet on the other hand, you too have gone through various phases in this respect, you were perhaps cheerier before your children

(I especially) disappointed and depressed you at home (you were quite different when visitors came), and you have perhaps become cheerier again, now that your grandchildren and your son-in-law show you some of the warmth that your own children, except perhaps Valli,* never could.

In any case, we were so different, and in our differences such a danger to each other that, had anyone wanted to predict how I, the slowly developing child, and you, the fully-grown man, would behave towards one another, they could have presumed that you would simply trample me underfoot until nothing of me remained. Well, that did not happen, what happens in life cannot be predicted, but maybe something even worse happened. In saying this, I ask you not to forget that I in no way find you guilty. Your effect on me was the effect you could not help having, but you should stop considering it some particular perversity on my part that I succumbed to that effect.

I was an anxious child, and yet I am sure I was also disobedient, as children are, I am sure that Mother spoilt me too, but I cannot believe that I was particularly difficult to handle, I cannot believe that you, by directing a friendly word my way, by quietly taking my hand or by giving me a kind look, could not have got everything you wanted from me. And you are fundamentally a kind and tender person (what follows does not contradict that, after all it refers only to how I saw you as a child) but not every child has the tenacity and fearlessness to search until he finds the kindness within. You, Father, are only capable of treating a child with the same means by which you were moulded, with vigour, noise and fits of rage, and in my case you found these means especially appropriate because you wanted to bring me up to be a strong, courageous boy.

Of course, I cannot accurately recall and describe your way of bringing me up in the very early years, but I can form some idea of it, drawing on my more recent experience and on your treatment of Felix. In doing this I am increasingly aware that you were younger then, therefore fresher, wilder, more natural and carefree than you are today, and that in addition you were largely occupied with the business, meaning you barely had time to see me once a day, so the impression you made on me would have been all the greater, and virtually impossible for me to become accustomed to.

There is only one episode from those early years that I remember directly, perhaps you remember it too. I was whining persistently for water one night, certainly not because I was thirsty, but in all probability partly to be annoying, partly to amuse myself. After a number of fierce threats had failed, you lifted me out of my bed, carried me out onto the *pavlatche** and left me awhile all alone, standing outside the locked door in my nightshirt. I do not mean to say that this was wrong of you, perhaps at that time there really was no other way of having a peaceful night, but I mention it as a characteristic example of the way you brought me up and the effect it had on me. This incident almost certainly made me obedient for a time, but it damaged me on the inside. I was by nature unable to reconcile the simple act (as it seemed to me) of casually asking for water with the utter horror of being carried outside. Years later it still tormented me that this giant man, my father, the ultimate authority, could enter my room at any time and, almost unprovoked, carry me from my bed out onto the pavlatche, and that I meant so little to him.

That was merely the beginning of things, but this feeling of powerlessness which still regularly overcomes me (in other respects admittedly a noble and productive feeling) stems in many ways from how you treated me. What I needed was a little encouragement, a little friendliness, a little help to keep my future open, instead you obstructed it, admittedly with the good intention of persuading me to go down a different path. But I was not fit for the path you chose. You encouraged me, for example, whenever I saluted or marched well, but I was no budding soldier, or you encouraged me when I could bring myself to eat heartily, especially when I drank beer, or when I managed to sing songs that I did not understand, or to parrot your own favourite clichés back to you, but none of it had a place in my future. And even today, it is typical of you only to encourage me in something when it engages your interest, when your own self-esteem is at stake, threatened either by me (for example with my marriage plans) or by others through me (for example when Pepa* insults me). Then you give me encouragement, remind me of what I am worth, what sort of woman I could marry, and condemn Pepa out of hand. But apart from the fact that I am, even at my present age, already virtually impervious to encouragement, I have to ask myself what good it could do me anyway, as it is only ever offered when I am not its primary object.

At that time, and throughout all that time, what I really needed was encouragement. I was already weighed down by your sheer bodily presence. I remember, for example, how we often undressed together in the same cubicle. I skinny, frail, fragile, you strong, tall, thickset. Even in the cubicle I felt a puny wretch, and not only in front of you but in front of the whole world, because for me you were the measure of all things. But when we stepped out before all the people, I with my hand in yours, a little skeleton, unsteady and barefoot on the planks, afraid of the water, unable to copy your swimming strokes which you kept on demonstrating with the best of intentions but actually to my profound shame, then I would lose myself in despair and at such moments all my past failures would come back to haunt me. I felt happiest when you sometimes undressed first and I could stay in the cubicle alone and delay the shame of my public appearance until you finally came looking for me and forced me to leave the cubicle. I was thankful to you for seeming not to sense my despair, besides, I was proud of my father's body. Incidentally, this difference between us remains much the same to this day.

Your intellectual domination had a similar effect on me. You had reached such heights, solely by your own efforts, that you had unbounded confidence in your own opinions. That was nowhere near so dazzling for me as a child, as it was for me later as a maturing young man. In your armchair you ruled the world. Your opinion was right, any other was mad, eccentric, *meshugge*,* not normal. In fact, your self-confidence was so great that you did not even have to be at all consistent, and could still never be wrong. It was even possible for you to have no opinion whatsoever on a matter, and in such cases all potential opinions on that matter had to be wrong without exception. You might rail against the Czechs, for example, then the Germans, then the Jews, and not only selectively but in all respects, and by the end of it you would be the only one left standing. You took on, for me, that enigmatic quality of all tyrants whose right to rule is founded on their identity rather than on reason. At least, it seemed that way to me.

Now, where I was concerned, you were in fact astonishingly often right, not only in conversation (and this would not have been surprising, for we hardly ever conversed), but also in reality. Although even that was not especially difficult to understand. I suffered, after all, in my every thought under intense pressure from you, even (and in fact especially) where my thoughts were completely different from yours. All these thoughts that seemed independent of you buckled from the outset under the burden of your derogatory judgments; for me to endure this and still to achieve the complete and lasting development of any thought was virtually impossible. I am not talking here of any lofty thoughts, rather of every little childhood undertaking. I had only to be happy about something or other, be inspired by it, come home and mention it and your response was an ironic sigh, a shake of the head, a finger rapping the table: "Is that what all the fuss is about?" or "I wish I had your worries!" or "What a waste of time!" or "That's nothing!" or "That won't put food on the table!" Naturally one could not expect you to be enthusiastic about every childish triviality, since you had your own worries. Even that was not the point. The point was rather that, thanks to your antagonistic nature, you disappointed the child with such determination and principle, and your antagonism constantly intensified as it accumulated material, until it became a permanent habit, even when your opinion was for once the same as mine, and these childhood disappointments were by the end not just everyday disappointments; but, since they concerned you, the measure of all things, they struck me to the very heart. Courage, resolution, confidence or delight in this and that could not long survive if you opposed it, or even if I could safely assume that you would oppose it; and this I could assume in practically every case.

This applied to people as well as thoughts. I only had to take a little interest in someone – which, given my nature, did not happen very often – for you, without any respect for my feelings or judgment, to weigh in with insults, slander and humiliation. Victims included such innocent, childlike people as the Yiddish actor Löwy.* Before you even knew him you compared him, in some dreadful way that I have already forgotten, to vermin and, as so often with people dear to me, you automatically had that proverb of the dogs and fleas* to hand. Here I remember the actor in particular because I made a note of what you said about him at the time: "This is how my father speaks about my friend (whom he does not even know), simply because he is my friend. I will always be able to reproach him with this whenever he accuses me of lacking a child's love and gratitude". I was never able to understand your complete obliviousness to the kind of grief and shame you could inflict on me with your words and judgments, it was as if you had no idea of your power. There can be no doubt that I, too, often hurt you with my words, but then I was always aware of it, it pained me but I could not

27

restrain myself, could not suppress the words, I would regret them even as I uttered them. You, on the other hand, lashed out with yours without a second thought, you felt sorry for nobody, either during or afterwards, people were left utterly defenceless.

But that was the way you brought me up. You have, I think, a gift for bringing up children; and such an upbringing could certainly have benefited someone like you; such a person would have grasped the reasoning behind what you told him, would not have concerned himself with other things and would quietly have done your bidding. For me as a child, though, everything you barked at me was as good as God's law, I never forgot it, it remained for me the most important means for judging the world, above all for judging you, and there you failed completely. Since as a child I was with you mainly at mealtimes, your lessons were for the most part lessons on correct table manners. Whatever was brought to the table had to be eaten up, the quality of the food was not to be mentioned – you, though, often found the meal uneatable, called it "swill", the "beast" (the cook) had ruined it. Because you, driven by your own predilection and sizeable appetite, ate everything fast, hot and in large mouthfuls, the child had to hurry, gloomy silence reigned at the table, interrupted by admonitions: "First eat, then speak" or "Faster, faster, faster" or "Look, see, I finished ages ago". We were not allowed to crunch bones, you were. We were not allowed to slurp vinegar, you were. The main thing was for the bread to be cut straight; but that you did so with a knife dripping with gravy was irrelevant. We had to take care not to let any scraps fall onto the floor, in the end they lay mostly under your seat. At the table we were to do nothing except eat, but you cleaned and trimmed your fingernails, sharpened pencils, dug in your ears with your toothpick. Please understand me correctly, Father, these would in themselves have been utterly insignificant details, they only came to depress me because they meant that you, a figure of such tremendous authority for me, did not yourself abide by the commandments you imposed. Hence there were for me three worlds, one where I lived, a slave under laws that had been invented solely for me and, moreover, with which I could never fully comply (I did not know why), then another world, infinitely distant from mine, in which you dwelt, busy with ruling, issuing orders and being angry when they were not obeyed, and finally a third realm where everybody else lived happily, free from orders and obligation. I was forever in disgrace, either I obeyed your orders, which was a disgrace for they applied, after all, only to me; or I was defiant, that was also a disgrace, for how dare I presume to defy you, or my reason for failing to obey was that I lacked, for example, your strength, your appetite, your aptitude, although you expected it of me as a matter of course; that was, in fact, the greatest disgrace of all. This was not how I thought as a child, but rather how I felt.

I see my situation at that time more clearly, perhaps, if I compare it with Felix's.* You treat him in a similar way, indeed you even employ a particularly fearful method of upbringing against him in that, whenever at mealtimes he does something you consider unclean, you do not content yourself, as you would with me, by saying, "What a pig you are," but add "A true Hermann," or "Just like your father." Now, this may perhaps – one cannot say more than "perhaps" – not really harm Felix a great deal, since for him you are no more than a grandfather, albeit an especially important one, certainly not everything as you were for me, moreover Felix is a quiet, even already to some extent manly character who may be bewildered by a thunderous voice, but not permanently affected by it, and above all he is relatively seldom in your company, he is subject to other influences, you are for him rather something of a lovable curiosity from whom he can pick and choose whatever he wants. For me you were nothing like a curiosity, I could not pick or choose, I had to accept everything.

And, what is more, without being able to voice any objection, for you are completely incapable of having a calm discussion on any topic that you do not approve of, or indeed one that you have not yourself raised; your imperious temperament prohibits it.

In recent years you have blamed this on your heart condition, in reality I do not know that you were ever any different, your heart condition is at the very least a means by which you dominate more absolutely, as the mere thought of it is enough to stifle any contradiction. Naturally I am not reproaching you for this, I am merely establishing a fact. You used to say for example: "There is simply no reasoning with her,* she flies in your face regardless", but in fact it was never she who attacked first; you tend to confuse issues with people; the issue under discussion flies in your face and you react to it without even listening to the person; whatever is said with hindsight can only aggravate you further, never change your mind. All you can then say is: "Do what you want; as far as I'm concerned it's your choice; you're old enough; it's not for me to give you advice" – and all that spoken with the awful hoarse undertone of anger and utter condemnation that admittedly makes me shudder less today than in my childhood, but only because the sense of guilt that so pervasively consumed me as a child has since been superseded in part by insight into the helplessness we shared.

Our inability to get on calmly had one more very natural consequence: I lost the ability to speak. I probably never would have turned out to be a great speaker in any case, but I would at least have grasped language to a normal degree of fluency. However, you forbade me to speak from a very early age: your threat, "Not a word in contradiction!" together with the image of your raised hand, has haunted me ever since I can remember. In your presence – for you are, when on familiar ground, an excellent speaker – I stuttered and spluttered, that angered you too, in the end I stopped speaking, perhaps at first in defiance, but gradually because I really was no longer able to think or speak in your presence. And because you were present throughout my upbringing, this went on to affect every aspect of my life. In any case, you are curiously mistaken if you believe that I was bent on disobeying you. "Persistent contrariness" was really never my guiding principle where you were concerned, as you believe and reproach me for. On the contrary: if I had tried less hard to follow you, I am sure you would have been much more satisfied with the result. As it is, the steps you took to discipline me always hit their target; I could never escape you; what I have now become, I have become (excepting my innate disposition and any external influences, of course) through the combination of your upbringing and my obedience. If the result embarrasses you in spite of this, if you unconsciously refuse to accept that it is the result of your upbringing, then it is precisely because your method and my substance were at such odds with one another. When you said, "Not a word in contradiction!" you meant only to silence in me that opposition which you found objectionable, but your influence in this respect was much too strong for me, I was *too* obedient, I fell completely silent, crept anxiously away from you and only dared speak when I was so far away that your power could no longer reach me, at least not directly. You looked on and saw deliberate "contrariness" in everything, but in reality it was only an inevitable consequence of your strength and my weakness.

The rhetorical devices you used in bringing me up, which were extremely effective, and at least in my case never failed, included: insults, threats, irony, spiteful laughter and – strangely – self-pity.

I cannot remember your ever having abused me directly or explicitly. Nor was that necessary, you had so many other methods, and besides, conversation at home, or particularly in the shop, brought the abuses you directed at others flying around my head in such abundance that I was sometimes almost stunned by them as a young boy, and had no reason not to apply them to myself, as the people you abused were certainly no worse than me, and you were certainly no more dissatisfied with them than you were with me. And here I saw further evidence of your enigmatic innocence and impregnability, you would abuse people without reservation or misgiving, yet you criticized anyone else who used abusive language, and forbade it.

You intensified your abuse with threats, and these some-times *were* aimed at me. I found this one particularly terrifying: "I'll gut you like a fish" – of course I knew that nothing worse would follow (as a small child, admittedly, I did not know that) but it tallied with my impression of your strength that you would have been capable of it. It terrified me too when you ran around the table screaming, trying to catch one of us, you obviously had no intention of catching us but still pretended, until Mother would eventually step in to rescue us. As the child's life had been spared only by your mercy, or so it seemed, it was to be duly lived out as an undeserved present from you. The same can be said of your threats concerning the consequences of disobedience. Whenever I embarked on something that you disapproved of and you threatened me with failure, my respect for your opinion was such that my failure became inevitable, even if I could perhaps defer it for a while. I lost faith in my own abilities. I became erratic, doubting. The older I grew, the more I provided you with evidence of my worthlessness, gradually you really came, in certain respects, to be right about me. Here I must be careful not to claim that I only became like this because of you; you merely intensified what was already there, but you intensified it greatly, simply because you held so much power over me and used this power to its full extent.

You set particular store by the use of irony in bringing me up, it was also especially fitting given your superiority over me. You usually reprimanded me like this: "Can't you do it this way instead? Isn't that a bit too much for you? Surely you don't have time for that?" or similar. And all of these questions were accompanied by a spiteful laugh and spiteful face. You punished me sometimes even before I knew what I had done wrong. When you particularly wanted to antagonize me you would refer to me in the third person, as if I were not even worthy of an angry address; you would say ostensibly to Mother, but actually to me as I sat there too, something like: "We simply can't have that kind of behaviour from our son" (This produced a counter habit in me: I never dared, or later never even thought, out of sheer habit, to address you directly while Mother was present. It was far less dangerous for me to put questions to Mother as long as she sat beside you, so I would ask Mother: "How is Father?", thus protecting myself from any surprises). Of course, there were times when I agreed with your extreme irony, notably when its target was someone else, Elli for example, with whom I had been on bad terms for years. For me it was an orgy of malice and *Schadenfreude* when you referred to her like this at almost every meal: "Look at the fat cow, she has to sit ten metres from the table", and again when you imitated her, in spiteful and exaggerated fashion as you sat in your chair, without the faintest hint of warmth or humour, but rather with bitter enmity, as if trying to show how terribly she offended your sensibilities. How often scenes like this must have occurred, and how little they actually achieved. This, I think, was because the extent of your anger and spite was so disproportionate to the matter in hand, we felt that your anger could not actually have been caused by such a trivial thing as sitting so far from the table, rather it must have been latent in you from the beginning, triggered in this case purely by chance. Since we were convinced that it would eventually be triggered anyway, we did not really let it trouble us, we were also desensitized by your constant threats; little by little we gradually became virtually certain that there was no danger of a real thrashing. We became surly, unobservant, disobedient children, constantly preoccupied with escape, mostly internal escape. And so you suffered, and we suffered. In your opinion you were doing no wrong when you stood there with clenched teeth and that gurgling laugh which had given me my first idea of hell as a child, and said bitterly (as you did recently on receiving a letter from Constantinople): "What a rabble!"

It seemed entirely incompatible with this attitude to your children that you should complain publicly – which you did very frequently. I admit that as a child (and probably later too) I was insensitive enough not to understand how you could ever expect to find sympathy. You were so immense in every respect, why should our sympathy or even our help be of concern to you? Indeed you surely would have scorned it, as you so often scorned us. For this reason I refused to believe that your complaints could be genuine, and searched for some hidden motive behind them. It was only later that I grasped how truly you suffered at the hands of your children, but while under different circumstances your complaints could still have prompted in me a childlike, open, unhesitating willingness to help, as things were I could never see them as anything other than transparent tools of teaching and humiliation, not very effective in themselves, but with the damaging side effect, to which I grew accustomed as a child, that the things I should have taken most seriously would be precisely those that I did not learn to take seriously enough.

Fortunately there were some exceptions to this, mostly when you suffered in silence, and your love and goodness joined forces to succeed in moving me, in spite of all the obstacles. This was admittedly rare, but it was wonderful. For instance whenever I saw you exhausted and nodding off in the shop on hot summer afternoons, elbows on the desk, or on Sundays when you came running to us breathless in the fresh summery weather; or once when Mother was seriously ill and I witnessed you shaking with tears, steadying yourself by the bookcase; or the last time I was ill and you came silently to me in Ottla's room, standing in the doorway and merely peering round to see me in bed, acknowledging me with a single considerate gesture of your hand. At times like these I lay back and cried with happiness, and I am crying again now as I write these lines.

You also have a particularly wonderful, very rare sort of serene, satisfied, approving smile that can make a person truly happy. I cannot remember any particular occasion on which you bestowed it on me as a child, but it probably happened at some stage, I see no reason why you would have refused it to me then, when I was still innocent in your eyes, besides which I was your greatest hope. Incidentally, even such friendly gestures have in the long term served only to intensify my guilt and make the world even harder to understand.

I preferred to rely on what was real and permanent. In order to assert myself a little against you, partly also out of a sort of revenge, I soon began to observe, collect and exaggerate all the little absurdities in your behaviour. For example, how you would be easily dazzled by certain people, for instance some Imperial Councillor, who for the most part only gave the illusion of being superior in rank to you, and how you would go on and on about them (on the other hand it also hurt me that you, my father, thought you needed such insignificant confirmations of your worth and bragged about them so much). Or I observed your predilection for those crude expressions, which you bellowed at maximum volume and followed with a laugh that suggested you thought you had said something particularly splendid, when in reality it had been only a feeble, uninspired obscenity (this was at the same time yet another humiliating manifestation of your vigour). Of course I made many diverse observations of this kind; they made me happy, they were a rare cause for exuberance and laughter, you noticed this sometimes and grew angry, thought it was spite, disrespect, but I can assure you, for me it was nothing more than an attempt – an ineffectual attempt – at self-preservation, they were the sort of jokes one makes about gods and kings, jokes that not only are linked to a deep respect, but indeed form an integral part of it.

Incidentally, you made your own attempts to defend yourself against me, as befitted our reciprocal situation. You used to point out how excessively well I lived and how well I was really treated. Though these observations were correct, I do not believe that they did me any appreciable good under the circumstances.

It is true that Mother was boundlessly good to me, but I could only see her treatment of me in relation to yours, that is to say, negatively. Mother unconsciously played the role of beater in the hunt. Whenever, in some improbable situation, the way you brought me up might have made me stand on my own two feet by instilling in me defiance, aversion or even hatred, Mother would offset it with gentleness and reasonableness (in the chaos of my childhood she was the epitome of reason), she pleaded my case and I was driven back into your orbit, from which I perhaps otherwise would have escaped to the advantage of us both. At other times there was no reconciliation, Mother simply protected me from you in secret, gave me something in secret, allowed me something, then in your eyes I was again that shady, lying, guilt-ridden creature that in his worthlessness could only get through devious means what he thought himself entitled to. Of course, I grew accustomed to seek by these means even what I thought I was not entitled to. This served still further to intensify my feelings of guilt.

It is also true that you hardly ever really beat me. But the way you screamed and went red in the face, the way you hastily undid your braces and hung them over the back of a chair – this was almost worse for me. Imagine a man who is about to be hanged. Hang him and he is dead, it is all over. But force him to witness all the preparations for his hanging and inform him of his reprieve only once the noose is dangling in front of his face, and you can make him suffer for the rest of his life. Something else, too, grew out of these many occasions where, in your clearly expressed opinion, I deserved a thrashing but was spared by your mercy – again, intense feelings of guilt. From every side, I was in your debt.

From the very beginning you reproached me (both in private and in front of others; you had no idea how this humiliated me, your children's affairs were always public) with living an easy life in peace, warmth and plenitude, all at your expense.

I am referring here to those remarks that must literally have become etched in my mind, such as: "When I was no more than seven I had to push the cart from village to village". "We all had to sleep in one room". "We counted ourselves lucky when we got potatoes". "For years my legs were covered in open sores for want of warm clothing". "When I was just a little boy I was sent away to work in a shop in Pisek".* "My parents never sent me anything, not even in the army, but still I sent money back home". "But in spite, in spite of everything – my father was still my father. Nobody appreciates that these days! What do these children know? Nobody's been through what I have! What child can understand that today?" Under different circumstances, anecdotes like these could have been an excellent way of teaching me, they could have given me strength and encouragement to survive the same trials and deprivations that my father had endured. But that was not at all what you wanted, you had taken care to make my situation quite different, there was never an opportunity for me to distinguish myself as you had done. Such an opportunity could only have been achieved by violence and upheaval, I would have had to break away from home (assuming that I had had the strength and resolve to do so, and that Mother for her part had not tried to prevent it by other means). But that was not at all what you wanted, you called it ingratitude, self-importance, disobedience, betrayal, madness. So while on the one hand you tempted me into it through your example, anecdotes and humiliation, you forbade it with the utmost severity on the other. Otherwise, apart from the incidental circumstances, you would surely have been charmed by Ottla's adventure in Zürau. She wanted to experience the countryside where you had grown up, she wanted work and deprivation as you had had them, she did not want to relax and enjoy the fruits of your hard work, just as you had been independent from your own father. Were those such terrible aspirations? So far from your own example and teaching? Admittedly, Ottla's aspirations failed ultimately in practice, were perhaps a little ridiculous, were carried out too ostentatiously, she showed too little consideration for her parents. But was she entirely to blame, could you not also blame her circumstances and particularly the fact that you and she were on such bad terms? Had she really been (as you have subsequently tried to convince yourself) any less of a stranger to you in the family home and business than she was later in Zürau? And was it not within your power (had you only found it in you) to turn that escapade into something much more positive through encouragement, guidance and support, or perhaps even simply through tolerance?

In connection with such experiences, you used to say in bitter jest that we had it too easy. But in a sense this was no joke at all. What you had had to fight for, we were given straight from your hand; but that struggle for an independent life which was granted to you from the beginning and which, of course, even we cannot entirely avoid, that is a privilege for which we are forced to strive belatedly, as adults with the strength of mere children. I am not saying that this necessarily makes our situation harder than yours, rather the two are probably equal (in saying this I do not mean to compare their basic natures), our only disadvantage is that we cannot use our deprivation to glorify ourselves or to belittle others, as you did with your deprivation. Nor do I deny that it would have been possible for me to have truly enjoyed the fruits of your great and successful work, made good use of them and, to your delight, developed them further, but for our alienation preventing it. As it was, I could enjoy what you gave me, but only with embarrassment, weariness, weakness, a sense of guilt. And that is why I could only ever receive your approbation with beggarly gratitude, I could never do anything to deserve it.

The next outward result of my whole upbringing was that I ran away from everything that even remotely reminded me of you. Firstly the business. As a street shop it should have delighted me, particularly in my childhood, it was so lively, lit up in the evenings, I saw and heard so much, could help here and there, show my skills, but above all I could marvel at your great talent for business, how you sold things, dealt with people, made jokes, never tired, immediately knew what to do in a difficult situation etc.; even the way you packaged goods or opened a box was a spectacle worth watching and the whole thing was, all in all, certainly not the worst education for a child. But as you came to scare me, gradually and in every respect, and as I became unable to distinguish you from the shop, I no longer felt comfortable even there. Things there that I had initially taken for granted came to torment and embarrass me, particularly your treatment of the staff. I do not know, perhaps it was normal for staff to be treated that way in the workplace (things were certainly similar during my term at the Assicurazioni Generali* for example, I justified my resignation to the manager, not entirely truthfully but on the other hand not completely deceitfully, by claiming that the abuse, of which I was incidentally not the direct target, was unbearable; my home life had left me too painfully sensitive to it), but as a child I was not concerned with other workplaces. I saw only you, screaming, shouting abuse and raging about the shop, something which I could not believe ever happened elsewhere in the world. And there was not only verbal abuse, but other sorts of tyranny too. For example, when you wanted certain goods not to be confused with others and, to prove your point, sent them flying from the counter with a single swipe – only the blindness of your rage excused you slightly – and the clerk would have to pick them up. Or your constant way of talking about one particular tuberculosis-stricken clerk: "The cripple should hurry up and die". You called the employees "paid enemies", and so they were, but even before they turned against you, you seemed to me to be their "paying enemy". This also taught me the important lesson that you could be unfair; I would not have noticed it so soon on my own, I was too overcome with guilt, which led me to convince myself that you were right; but these people were, in my childhood opinion (later a little but not very much altered) complete strangers who nonetheless worked for us and who, for all that, had to live in continual fear of you. Of course I exaggerated the situation because I wrongly assumed that you were as frightening to others as you were to me. If that had been the case, they really would have been unable to cope; but since they were grown adults with mostly excellent nerves, they shrugged off your insults effortlessly and you actually suffered far worse than they did. For me, however, it made the shop unbearable, it reminded me all too acutely of my relationship with you: quite apart from your interest as an employer and quite apart from your need to dominate, you were so superior as a businessman to all who ever learnt from you that none of their achievements could ever satisfy you, and I likewise must have disappointed you on a continual basis. Because of this, I could not help but ally myself with the staff, also incidentally because, through my timidity, I could not understand how someone could insult a stranger like that, and this timidity made me want somehow, for my own safety, to reconcile the staff with you, with our family, for I thought they must be terribly outraged. In trying to achieve this it was no longer enough to treat the staff with normal politeness, nor even with modesty, rather I had to show humility, not only did I have to greet them at every opportunity, where possible I also had to decline a greeting in return. And if I, insignificant as I was, had licked the soles of their feet, it still could not have made up for the way in which you, the master, attacked them from on high. My tendency to form this kind of relationship with other people affected me beyond the shop and into my future (Ottla demonstrates a comparable, if a less dangerous and far-reaching phenomenon, in her keen involvement with the poor for example, in the way in which, to your great annoyance, she would insist on sitting with the serving girls, and so on). By the end I was almost afraid of the shop and it certainly ceased appealing to me long before I started school and became increasingly distant from it. Furthermore, my skills did not seem up to the job, since even yours, as you admitted, were inadequate. You then tried (which moves and shames me still) to turn my aversion for the shop into some degree of affection for you, for your work, by maintaining that I lacked business sense, that my head was made for loftier ideas etc. Of course this contrived explanation pleased

Mother, and even I, in my vanity and need, allowed myself to believe it. Had it really been purely or mostly "loftier ideas" that had come between me and the business (which I now, but only now, truly and honestly hate), they would surely have manifested themselves differently, they would not have allowed me to drift quietly and anxiously through school and legal studies, until I ended up behind a civil servant's desk.

If I wanted to escape you, I would have had to escape the rest of the family too, even Mother. Of course she always gave me protection, but only in relation to you. She loved you too much and was too faithfully devoted to you, for her to be an independent source of moral support in my longer-term struggle as a child. Moreover, my childhood instinct was right, for over the years Mother became even more closely allied to you; where she had once retained some independence in her own affairs, ably and quietly, within the narrowest limits so as not to anger you too much, over the years she began more and more blindly to accept the way you judged and condemned your children, more out of emotional sympathy than rational agreement with you, and especially in Ottla's case, which was the most difficult one. Of course, we must remember what a punishing and utterly exhausting position Mother held in the family. She slaved away in the shop and at home, suffered doubly through all the family illnesses, but most of all she suffered in her role as mediator between us and you. You always treated her with love and consideration, but in this respect you spared her no more than we spared her. We hammered away at her without consideration, you from your side, we from ours. We only did it to amuse ourselves, we could not see how it hurt her, we could not see beyond the war that we waged on you, you on us, and we were happy to vent our frustration on her. It further damaged our upbringing that you – of course without being the slightest bit at fault – punished her instead of us. It even seemed to justify the otherwise unjustifiable way we treated her. How she suffered at our hands because of you and at your hands because of us, not to mention those times when you were in the right because she was spoiling us, even if this "spoiling" may sometimes have been nothing but a silent, unconscious retaliation on her part against your system. Of course, all this would have been unbearable for Mother, had her love for us, and her happiness in that love, not given her the strength to bear it.

My sisters were only partially on my side. Happiest in her relationship with you was Valli. The closest of us all to Mother, she submitted to you in much the same way without it costing her much effort or causing her much harm. But you accepted her more readily too, despite her relative lack of Kafka-like attributes, because she reminded you of Mother. Or perhaps her lack of Kafka-like attributes even suited you;

where there were none, even you could not demand them; furthermore it relieved you of the feeling that something had gone astray and required salvaging by force. Besides, you may never particularly have liked the way that Kafka-like features manifested themselves in women. Valli's relationship with you might have grown stronger still, had the rest of us not spoilt it somewhat.

Elli is the only one of us to have almost completely succeeded in breaking free of your influence – just what I would least have expected from her in her childhood. She was such a clumsy, tired, anxious, morose, guilt-ridden, self-effacing, spiteful, lazy, greedy, miserly child, I could hardly bring myself to look at her, she reminded me so much of myself, she was so greatly influenced by the way you brought us up, as I was. Her avarice was particularly repulsive to me, since mine was, if possible, even worse. Avarice is after all one of the surest signs of deep unhappiness; I was so uncertain of everything that I could only be sure of possessing what I held between my hands or lips, or what was at least on its way there, and it was precisely these things that she, in a position similar to mine, delighted in taking away from me. But this all changed when, still in her youth – that was the most important factor – she left home, married, had children, became cheerful, carefree, spirited, generous, selfless, hopeful. It is almost inconceivable that you failed to notice this change, you certainly did not consider it praiseworthy, you were so blinded by the resentment you always felt for Elli and which still remains essentially unchanged, even if it has become far less acute now that Elli no longer lives with us, besides which it has been lessened by your love for Felix and affection for Karl.* Only Gerti* still occasionally has to suffer for it.

I hardly dare write about Ottla, I know that in doing so I jeopardize everything I hoped to achieve with this letter. Under normal circumstances, I mean when she is in no real need or danger, you have nothing but contempt for her; you even admitted to me that you think she deliberately causes you constant grief and anger, and that while you suffer on her account, she is happy and contented. A sort of devil. What a monstrous rift there must be between you and her, even greater than the one between you and me, to engender such a monstrous misunderstanding. She is so distant from you that you barely see her any more, but instead see a ghost in her place. I admit that you found her particularly difficult. I cannot make complete sense of this very complicated state of affairs, but in any case here was a sort of Löwy equipped with the best Kafka-like weapons. I was no real match for you; you soon disposed of me; all that then remained was escape, bitterness, grief, inner struggle. You two, on the other hand, were constantly ready for battle, constantly fresh, constantly full of energy. A sight as great as it was hopeless. At the very beginning you were certainly very close, for even today Ottla is perhaps the purest emblem of your marriage to Mother and of the power implicit in that marriage. I do not know what put an end to that happy harmony between father and child, I can only assume that her situation developed in a similar way to mine. With you behaving tyrannically, and she demonstrating a Löwy-like defiance, sensitivity, sense of justice, restlessness, and all this reinforced through an awareness of her Kafka-like strength. I probably influenced her too, but hardly deliberately, rather simply by being there. Moreover, as the last-born, she entered into a pre-established family dynamic and was able to form her own judgment from the ample material already there. I can even believe that she hesitated to do this for a while, considering whether she should throw herself at your feet or your opponents', clearly you neglected something at that time and pushed her away, otherwise you would have become a splendidly harmonious pair. Although I would have lost an ally in this pairing, the sight of you together would have been rich compensation, and moreover the immeasurable happiness of finding complete satisfaction in at least one child would have altered you significantly in my favour. That, however, is now no more than a dream. Ottla has no contact with her father, she must follow her own path like I do, and the additional confidence, self-assurance, good health, lack of scruples that she has compared with me makes her even more spiteful and treacherous in your eyes. That I understand; seen from your point of view, she could not appear otherwise. Indeed, even she is capable of looking at herself from your perspective, empathizing with you, fretting – not despairing, despair is my speciality – about the situation. Although you often see us together, in apparent contradiction to all I have said – we whisper, laugh, from time to time you hear us mention you. You see us as insolent conspirators. An odd sort of conspirators. Admittedly you are a prominent subject of our conversations, as you have been of our thoughts since the very beginning, however, we do not come together with the intention of plotting against you, but rather to talk through with one another – in every detail, from all angles, at every opportunity, from near and far, under stress, in jest, in sincerity, with love, defiance, anger, revulsion, resignation, guilt, with all the strength of our heads and hearts – that terrible trial that hangs over us and separates us from you, a trial in which you always claim the role of judge although, at least for the most part (here I admit I may make many mistakes), you are just as weak and blinded as we are.

Irma* is a particularly enlightening example in this whole saga of how you brought people up. On the one hand admittedly she was an outsider, she only entered the business as an adult, dealt with you mostly as her boss and was therefore exposed to your influence in smaller doses, at an age when she was already capable of resistance; on the other hand she was also a blood relation, she admired in you her father's brother, and your power over her was far greater than that of a boss. And despite this she, who even in her bodily frailty was so competent, clever, diligent, modest, trustworthy, selfless, faithful, who loved you as an uncle and admired you as a boss, who proved her worth in other posts before and since – never made you a very good employee. In her relationship with you she was like another child, of course we helped to push her in that direction, and the buckling power of your presence weighed down on her to such a degree that she developed (admittedly only in your presence and hopefully without the deeper suffering of a child) a forgetfulness, thoughtlessness, morbid humour, perhaps even a little defiance as far as she was capable of it, although here I take no account of her sickly disposition, general low spirits and the burden of dreary domesticity that she shouldered. The complex implications of your relationship with her were summed up by you in a single, almost blasphemous sentence that nevertheless became a classic for us, it proved your obliviousness to the way you treated people: "She died and left me in a real mess".

I could describe the wider implications of your influence and my struggle against it, but I would be treading on un-certain ground, besides the further you moved away from the business and family, the friendlier, more accommodating, politer, more considerate, more involved (outwardly as well as inwardly) you became, just like an autocrat who steps outside his own land, who no longer has any reason to be tyrannical all the time and can associate affably with even the lowliest of people. In the group photographs from Franzensbad, for example, you stood tall and merry among the surly creatures, like a king on his travels. Of course even your children could have thrived on this, had they only been able to recognize it as children, which was in fact impossible, and I, for instance, would not have been so eternally confined to the innermost, strictest, suffocating sphere of your influence, as I was in reality.

Through this I not only lost my sense of family as you see it, on the contrary I still had a sense of the family, indeed a largely negative one, and of inner detachment from you, which could of course never succeed. But my relationships with people outside the family suffered perhaps even more under your influence. You are entirely wrong if you believe that I do all I can for other people out of love and devotion, nothing for you or the family out of coldness and betrayal. I repeat for the tenth time: I probably would have turned out to be an anxious person in any case, shy of people in general, but it is a long, dark path from there to where I actually ended up. (Until this point in the letter I have made relatively few deliberate omissions, but now and later I will have to omit certain things that are too hard for me to confess – to you and to myself. I say this so that you do not believe, should the overall picture be a little unclear in places, that I lack evidence. On the contrary, evidence exists that could create too unbearably crude a picture. It is not easy to find a middle ground here.) It will suffice in this case, incidentally, to cast our minds back: I had lost my self-confidence whenever I was in your presence, had exchanged it for a boundless sense of guilt (I was thinking of this boundlessness when I once summed it up perfectly in relation to someone else: "He is afraid that the shame will outlive him."). I could not suddenly transform myself when I came into contact with other people, rather I developed a deeper sense of guilt towards them, because as I have already said, I felt compelled to make amends for the way that you had treated them in the business, something for which I felt jointly responsible. Moreover, you objected secretly or openly to everyone with whom I associated, and I was obliged to rectify this too. The mistrust for people in general that you tried to teach me at work and at home (name a single person of any importance to me as a child whom you did not roundly criticize on at least one occasion), and that strangely did not weigh on you at all (you were strong enough to bear it, besides which it may purely have been an emblem of your dominance) – that mistrust, which was never justified in my childlike eyes, as I saw around me only inimitably excellent people, that mistrust developed within me into mistrust of myself, and a perpetual fear of all other people. And so in this respect I was generally unable to save myself from you. You deceived yourself on this front, perhaps because you truly *were* unaware of my involvement with people and assumed, suspiciously and jealously (am I denying that you love me?) that I had to compensate for my lack of family life elsewhere, as it was impossible for me to live like that away from home. Incidentally, as a child I found one certain comfort in all this, a comfort in distrust of my own judgment; I told myself: "You exaggerate, you think of every little triviality as if it were a great anomaly, the way young people always do." I later almost completely lost this comfort, however, when I came to understand the world better.

I found just as little escape from you in Judaism. Escape would have been perfectly possible here, or rather, it would have been possible for us both to find each other in Judaism, or at least to find a starting point for our union. But what a version of Judaism you taught me! Over the years I have viewed it in three different ways.

As a child I reproached myself, as you reproached me, for not going to synagogue enough, not fasting etc. I believed I was wronging not myself but you, and guilt, in ever-ready supply, consumed me.

Later as a young man, I failed to understand how you, given your negligible commitment to Judaism, could reproach me for not striving (even for the sake of piety, as you put it) to show the same negligible commitment. It really was, as far as I could see, negligible, a joke, not even a joke. You went to synagogue four times a year, there you resembled more, to say the least, the indifferent throng than the few who took it seriously, you patiently went through the prayers as a formality, sometimes astonished me with your ability to turn to the passage currently being recited from the prayer book, incidentally I was allowed, as long as I was in the synagogue (that was the main thing) to wander about as I pleased. And so I yawned and dozed my way through the many hours (in later years I believe I was only ever that bored again in dancing lessons) and tried to take as much delight as possible in the few little variations of the service, such as the opening of the Ark of the Covenant, which always reminded me of those shooting booths where a similar box would open its doors if someone hit the target, only there something interesting would emerge, while here it was always the same old headless dolls. Incidentally I was also very scared in the synagogue, not only, as one might expect, by the close contact with so many people, but also because you once casually mentioned that even I could be called upon to recite from the Torah. I dreaded that for

57

years. But apart from this my boredom knew no significant interruptions, the bar mitzvah came closest, but it required only risible rote-learning, leading to the risible climax of passing an examination and then, as far as you were concerned, to other insignificant events, for example when you were called to the Torah, a purely social undertaking in my eyes, and one in which you acquitted yourself well, or when you stayed behind in the synagogue to say prayers for the dead while I was banished, which, for a long time, clearly because of my banishment and lack of any deeper interest, evoked in me the more or less unconscious feeling that something indecent was going on. That was the state of things in the synagogue, at home it was, if at all possible, even more wretched, since worship was limited to the first Seder* which developed more and more into a side-splitting farce, admittedly under the influence of the growing children. (Why did you have to submit to this influence? Because you inspired it). Such were the religious beliefs I inherited from you, the only further addition being the way you extended your whole arm to point out "millionaire Fuchs's sons" whenever they accompanied their father to the synagogue on High Holy Days.* I did not know what to do with this inheritance, other than to reject it at the earliest opportunity; in the circumstances I felt rejection to be the most pious option.

Later still, though, I looked at it differently and understood why you believed I had spitefully betrayed you in this matter, as in so many others. You actually had brought some trace of Judaism with you from that little ghetto-like village community, it was not much and you lost another fraction of it during your time in the city and the army, but impressions and memories from your youth were still just enough to allow you to live some sort of Jewish life, particularly as you did not need much help to do that, you had a very strong sense of your roots and were virtually impervious to religious scruples on a personal level unless they were closely bound up with social scruples. Your life was essentially governed by your unequivocal belief in the opinions of a particular class of Jewish society and, since these opinions were a part of your identity, you came to believe unequivocally in yourself. Here too, there was enough Judaism, but it was too little to be handed down to a child, it seeped away even as you passed it on. Your impressions from your own youth were prevented from reaching the child, partly due to their inexpressible nature and partly due to your dreaded personality. It was also impossible to make the child understand, as he observed all too well out of sheer fear, that the few insignificant rituals carried out by you in the name of Judaism, with an indifference befitting their insignificance, could have a higher meaning. For you they meant something as small souvenirs from earlier times, and it was because of this that you wanted me to appreciate them, but as they no longer had any intrinsic worth even for you, you could only achieve this through persuasion or intimidation; on the one hand, this could never succeed and on the other, as you never recognized your weak position here, it had the unavoidable effect of making you angry with me for my apparent stubbornness.

This whole thing is, of course, no isolated phenomenon, something similar happened to a large part of that transitional generation of Jews migrating into the cities from a still relatively devout country; this happened automatically and inevitably, but it added to our particular relationship, already somewhat acrimonious, a further considerable degree of pain. Although you, like I, ought to believe in your innocence on this count, you should attribute that innocence to your nature and the conditions of the time, not merely to external circumstances, I mean you should not claim to have been prevented, by too much other work and strife, from concerning yourself with such things. You used, in this way, to turn the fact of your undeniable innocence into an unfair reproach towards others. Such reproaches are always very easily refuted, and this instance is no exception. You should have concerned yourself less with teaching your children a lesson, than with leading an exemplary life; had your Judaism been stronger, your example would in turn have been more compelling, this is self-evident and once again under no circumstances a reproach, but merely a defence against your reproaches. You recently read Franklin's* memoirs of his youth. In truth, I deliberately gave them to you to read, not, as you remarked ironically, because of a short passage about vegetarianism, but because of the author's description of his relationship with his father, and the incidental revelation of his relationship with his son, for whom the memoirs were indeed written. Here I do not intend to go into details.

This view of your Judaism received confirmation in retrospect, when you noticed my increased involvement with the faith. Now, you have always had an aversion to every one of my pursuits, especially to the way I develop an interest in things, and this was no exception. But beyond that, I might have had reason to hope that you would make a small exception in this case. After all, the Judaism stirring within me was born of your Judaism, and it brought with it an opportunity to forge new relations between us. I do not deny that, had you shown interest in these things, I may immediately have become wary of them. It does not occur to me at all to claim that I am somehow better than you in this respect. But it was never even put to the test. Judaism became loathsome to you because of the way it manifested itself in me, Jewish writings became unreadable, they "disgusted you". This could have been an insistence on your part that the only correct version of Judaism was the one you showed me in my childhood, that there was nothing beyond that. But the very notion that you could insist on such a thing was almost unthinkable. Otherwise the "disgust" (apart from the fact that it applied primarily not to Judaism, but to my character) could simply have meant that you unconsciously recognized the weakness of your Judaism and of my Jewish upbringing, did not want to be reminded of it in any way and reacted to all reminders with open hatred. Incidentally your negative esteem of my Judaism was vastly exaggerated; this Judaism bore your own curse within it, and its development was determined fundamentally, that is to say fatally, by my relationships with other people.

Your loathing dealt a heavier blow to my writing and everything that, even unknown to you, was related to it. Here I had in fact gained a little independent distance from you, even if in doing so I slightly resembled a worm, its tail pinned to the ground under somebody's foot, tearing loose from the front and wriggling away to the side. I was to some extent safe, I could breathe freely; the revulsion that you felt for my writing was, unusually, a relief to me. Although my vanity, my ambition suffered at the greeting (that came to be notorious for us) with which you welcomed my books: "Put it on my bedside table!" (you would normally be playing cards when a book came), despite this I was happy on the whole, not only out of rebellious spite, not only out of delight in this new confirmation of my analysis of our relationship, but on a much deeper level, since that phrase said to me: "You are free now!" Of course I was deceiving myself, I was not, or at best, not yet free. My writing was about you, all I did there was to lament what I could not lament on your shoulder. It was a deliberately long drawn-out parting from you, yet although you instigated it, I was able to choose its eventual direction. But how little all of that meant! This whole matter is only worthy of discussion to the extent that it features in my life, otherwise I would not even have mentioned it, and even more so because it has dominated my life, as a presentiment in my childhood, later as hope, still later often as despair, and it dictated – I might say once again in your image – the few small decisions I made.

My choice of career, for example. Of course, you gave me complete freedom to choose in your generous and, in this case, even patient way. Admittedly too, in this matter, you did no more than to treat your son in accordance with the general custom of the Jewish middle class, or at least the value judgments of this class, to which you attributed such great authority. A significant role was also played by your misunderstanding of my character. For you have always thought, influenced by fatherly pride, by ignorance of who I was, by the conclusions you drew from my feebleness, that I was particularly hard-working. In your opinion I spent my childhood constantly studying and my later life constantly writing. Now, that is not remotely true. Rather you might say, much less exaggeratedly, that I studied little and learnt nothing; it is not very surprising that something of my learning has survived the years, given my moderately good memory and my not altogether hopeless analytical ability, but in any case what is left in terms of knowledge, and especially the firmness of its grounding, is exceedingly pitiful by comparison with the amount of time and money spent in the course of an externally carefree, peaceful life, particularly too by comparison with almost everybody else I know. It is pitiful, but for me it is understandable. I have worried, for as long as I can recall, so deeply about asserting my spiritual existence that nothing else has ever mattered to me. Our Jewish grammar-school pupils are generally strange, they display the most unlikely characteristics, but the cold, barely concealed, unyielding, childishly helpless, almost ridiculous, wildly self-satisfied indifference of a self-sufficient but coldly imaginative child is something that I have only ever encountered in myself, admittedly in my case it was also the only protection against a nervous breakdown from anxiety and guilt. I worried only about myself, but I did so in a great variety of ways. Sometimes I worried about my health; it started imperceptibly enough, here and there a little apprehension about digestion, hair loss, spinal curvature etc., this escalated in countless gradations, before finishing up as a real illness. And what was all this? No actual physical illness. But since I could not be certain of anything, since I needed new validation of my existence with every passing second, since I was never in actual, absolute, sole possession of anything, as only I could determine unequivocally – in truth a disinherited son – because of all this I became uncertain even of what was nearest to me, my own body; I grew taller and taller at an alarming rate and had no idea how to cope with it, the burden was too heavy, my back grew crooked; I hardly dared move, let alone exercise, I remained weak; I was astonished that anything in me still functioned, as if it were a miracle, for instance my good digestion; this in itself was enough to destroy it, opening the way for all sorts of hypochondria, until eventually, under the superhuman demands of a desire to marry (I shall speak about this later) my lungs began to bleed, and here the apartment in Schönborn Palace* – which I needed only because I believed I needed it for my writing, so that it too is relevant here – may also have been responsible. So none of this came from working too hard, as you always imagined. There were years when, in full health, I lazed away more time on the sofa than you did in your whole lifetime, periods of sickness included. Whenever, frightfully busy, I hurried away from you, it was mostly to go and lie down in my room. The sum total of my achievements in the office (where laziness is rarely seen and was in any case kept in check by my nervousness) as well as at home was so meagre, if you knew the truth of it you would be horrified. By nature I am probably not at all lazy, but there was nothing for me to do. At home I was snubbed, denounced, defeated and although I made an enormous effort to escape and go elsewhere, that could not really be called work, for it was an impossible goal that with my poor strength, a few small exceptions aside, I could not attain.

It was in this state that I was given the freedom to choose my profession. But was I at all able to make use of such freedom? Did I still trust in my ability to enter a real profession? My appreciation of myself was much more dependent on you than on anything else, for instance any external success. Success merely strengthened me for a moment, nothing more, your weight, pulling me down the other way, was always much stronger. I was convinced I would never even get through the first year at school, but I succeeded, I was even awarded a prize; but I would certainly never pass the grammar-school entrance exam, yet again I succeeded; but then I would certainly fail my first year at that school, but no, I did not fail, in fact I kept on succeeding. But this did not give me confidence, on the contrary, I became convinced – and your disapproving face was formal proof of this – that the more I succeeded, the worse my eventual downfall would be. In my mind's eye I often saw the terrible staff meeting (school is merely the most integral example, but it was the same with other things all around me) after I had passed the first year, and in the second after I had passed that, and in the third etc., how they would assemble to examine this exceptional, scandalous case, how I, the most inept or at least the most ignorant pupil, could possibly have managed to creep my way up into this class, which would of course immediately spit me out now that all eyes were on me, to the delight of all those righteous people who were free of this nightmare. It is not easy for a child to live with fantasies like this. What did I care about lessons under these circumstances? Who would have been able to ignite a single spark of real interest in me? At this crucial age I was interested in lessons, and not only lessons but everything around me, much in the same way as a defaulting bank clerk, still employed and terrified of being found out, is interested in the routine little transactions that he must still carry out as an employee. Compared with that main concern, everything else was so insignificant, so distant. Things continued like this until my final exam, which to a certain extent I really did only pass through cheating, and then it all came to a halt and I was free. If I had been preoccupied with myself back then, despite the discipline of grammar school, how much more so now that I was free. This meant that I had no real freedom to choose my career, I knew that, compared with my main concern, I would again be as indifferent to everything as I was to the lessons taught at school, so I had as soon as possible to find a career that, without wounding my pride too much, would allow me to indulge this indifference. Law was the obvious choice. Little rebellious attempts at other things, spurred by vanity or blind hope, such as a fortnight's study of chemistry or half a year of German, served only to strengthen that essential conviction. And so I studied law, which meant that in the few months before the exams, even to such an extent that it damaged my nerves, my mind was positively living on sawdust, indeed on sawdust that had already been chewed for me by thousands of other mouths. But in a certain respect I liked it precisely because of this, just as in a certain respect I liked my earlier schooling and my later career as a civil servant, for it all suited my situation perfectly. At any rate I showed astonishing foresight, even as a small child I had abundantly clear presentiments about my studies and career. I expected no salvation from all of this, I had long given up all hope of salvation.

However, I showed almost no foresight at all where the significance and possibility of marriage were concerned; this, the most extreme terror of my life so far, came upon me almost completely unexpectedly. I had developed so slowly as a child, these things seemed utterly detached from me, now and then it was necessary to think about them; but it was not clear that this was to be a permanent, decisive test, and even the bitterest of all. In reality, however, my attempts at marriage turned out to be my most hopeful and spectacular attempts to escape you, and correspondingly their failure was every bit as spectacular.

I fear, because I always fail in this respect, that I shall here again fail to make you understand my attempts at marriage. And yet the success of this whole letter depends on it, for although on the one hand the attempts brought all my positive forces together, they also brought together, with a certain fury, all the negative forces in me that I described as resulting in part from the way you brought me up, and that raised a barrier between me and marriage, that is to say my weakness, my lack of self-confidence, my overwhelming sense of guilt. Explaining this will be even more difficult because I have mulled it all over and over for so many days and nights that the mere thought of it now confuses me. The explanation is only made easier by what I think is a complete misunderstanding of the issue on your part; the task of slightly correcting such a complete misunderstanding does not seem too difficult.

Firstly you put my failure to marry in the same category as my other failures; I would not have objected to that in itself, providing that you had accepted my above explanation for this failure. Indeed, it does belong in this category, but you underestimate the significance of it and underestimate it in such a way that, when we discuss it together, we are actually referring to completely different things. I dare say that in your whole life you never experienced anything that meant as much to you as my attempts at marriage did to me. In saying that, I do not mean you never experienced anything as important in itself, on the contrary, your life was much richer, more anxiety-ridden and busier than mine, but it is precisely for this reason that you never experienced anything of this sort. It is rather like one person having to climb five small steps, and another person only one step, but one that is as high as the first five put together; the former will not only conquer his five, but hundreds and thousands more, he will have led a great and very demanding life, but no single step of his journey will have meant as much to him as that one first step will have meant to the latter, the step that he, for all the strength in him, cannot climb, that he cannot scale, let alone of course progress beyond.

Marrying, founding a family, accepting all one's children, supporting them in this uncertain world and even guiding them a little is, in my opinion, the pinnacle of human achievement. The fact that so many people seem to succeed is no proof of the contrary, for firstly not many really do succeed, and secondly the success of the remaining few is, by and large, not due to any "action" on their part, rather it simply happens for them; their achievement in this case, though it does not reach that pinnacle, is very significant and very honourable (especially as it is not possible to differentiate entirely between an "action" and a "happening"). And nor, ultimately, is it a question of this pinnacle of achievement, but rather some far-removed yet respectable approximation to it; after all, a man does not need to fly right into the middle of the sun, he needs only to find his way into a little place on earth where the sun occasionally shines and provides some warmth.

But how was I prepared for all this? As badly as possible. This is apparent from what I have already said. Where preparing me directly as an individual and providing the basic necessities were concerned, you did not seem to interfere much. And it could not have been otherwise, here the general sexual customs of our class, our nationality and our time were the deciding factors. Yet you did intervene even here, not much, for such intervention presupposes strong mutual trust and we both lacked this, you intervened long before the critical time, and not very happily, because our needs were completely different; something that moves me does not necessarily affect you and vice versa, something you would consider innocent, I might consider reprehensible and vice versa, something of no consequence for you might be the final nail in my coffin.

I remember taking a walk with you and Mother one evening, it was around Josefsplatz* near what is now the international bank, when I started to talk about these matters of interest in a stupidly boastful manner, haughty, proud, detached (that was untrue), cold (that was genuine) and stuttering, as indeed was normally the case when I spoke with you, reproaching the two of you for having left me uninstructed, so that my classmates had had to enlighten me, for having exposed me to great dangers (here I was lying in my typical shameless manner to give the illusion of courage, for as a result of my anxious nature I had no real concept of these "great dangers" beyond the most routine sexual misdemeanours of city children), I implied by way of conclusion, however, that fortunately I now knew everything, that I needed no more advice and that everything was all right. I had started to talk about this chiefly because it amused me, at least to talk about it, then partly out of curiosity and finally also somehow to avenge myself on both of you for something or other. In keeping with your usual manner, you reacted very simply, merely said something to the effect that you could advise me on how to pursue these things safely. Perhaps it had been precisely my intention to provoke such an answer, it certainly tallied with my lascivious nature as a child who had been overfed with meat and all the good things in life, yet was still sexually inactive and constantly preoccupied with himself, but I felt such an outward sense of shame at this, or rather I believed that I ought to have done, that despite my wishes I was unable to speak with you about it ever again, and I broke off the conversation with arrogant impudence.

The answer you gave me is not easy to judge, on the one hand its brutal candour suggests a certain primitiveness, on the other hand, the unscrupulousness of the lesson it teaches is very modern. I do not remember how old I was at the time, certainly not much more than sixteen. For a boy like me, it was indeed a very strange answer and it illustrates the gulf between us that this was in fact the first explicit and comprehensive lesson on life you ever taught me. But its real meaning, which I understood even then but which I was not half-conscious of until later, was as follows: what you were advising me to do was, in your opinion and even in my own opinion at the time, the filthiest thing imaginable. Your efforts to ensure I would bring no physical trace of the filth home were neither here nor there, they served only to protect you, your house. What really mattered was the way in which you remained exempt from your own advice, a husband, a pure man, above such things; this was probably made worse for me at the time by the fact that it made even marriage seem indecent, preventing me from applying the information I had heard about marriage in general to my own parents. This made you even purer, exalted you even higher. The thought that you could have given yourself similar advice before you married was completely unthinkable to me. And so there was almost no trace of human filth left on you. And yet it was you who drove me down into this filth with your few frank words, as if I were destined for it. If the world had consisted only of me and you, an idea that I held very dear, then all the purity in the world would be embodied in you, and the filth, by dint of your advice, would be embodied in me. It was of course incomprehensible in itself that you could sentence me to such a thing, to me it was explicable only by old guilt and the deepest contempt on your part. Once again this dealt a blow, a very hard blow, to my innermost being.

It is perhaps here, too, that our guiltlessness, both yours and mine, becomes most clear. A gives B a piece of advice that is frank, in keeping with his approach to life, not very appealing but widely accepted in contemporary city life, and that will perhaps even help prevent damage to B's health. This advice is not morally very invigorating for B, but there is no reason why he should not be able to work his way out of it and repair the damage over the next few years, incidentally he is not at all obliged to take the advice and in any case the advice contains nothing which could cause B's whole future to collapse on him. And yet this is exactly the sort of thing that does happen, but only because you are A and I am B.

I have a particularly clear overview of this mutual guiltlessness because we clashed in a similar way under completely
different circumstances about twenty years later, which was
indeed horrendous but admittedly much less damaging in
itself, for what did I, at thirty-six years old, have left in me
to damage? I am talking about a minor discussion on one
of those tense days after I had told you of my latest plans to
marry. You said something like: "She probably put on some
sort of fancy blouse, as only those Prague Jewesses know how,
and of course you instantly decided to marry her. And with all
possible haste, within the week, tomorrow, today. I just don't
understand you, you're a fully grown man, you live in the
city, and still you know no better than to marry the first girl
that comes along. Can you really not see the alternatives? If
you're frightened, I'll go with you." Your words were clearer
and more detailed, but I cannot remember the particulars,
perhaps my eyes went a little blurred, I was concentrating
almost more on Mother who, although she completely agreed
with you, picked something up from the table and left the
room.

You have perhaps never humiliated me so deeply with
words, nor more clearly showed your contempt for me.
When you said similar words to me twenty years earlier, I
might from your perspective have seen some sort of respect
for the precocious city child, who in your opinion was already

fit to be initiated directly into the ways of the world. Today this consideration could only deepen your contempt, because the boy, who previously showed considerable courage, has since stagnated and appears not to have been enriched by any further experience, only made more wretched by the passing of twenty years. It meant nothing at all to you which girl I chose. You had always (unconsciously) held my ability to make decisions in low esteem and you now (unconsciously) thought you knew exactly what it was worth. You knew nothing of my attempts to escape by other means, you could not therefore know what thought processes had led me to this attempt at marriage, you could only guess and, in keeping with your general opinion of me, you imagined me to have the most loathsome, crude, risible motives. And you did not hesitate for a second to tell me as much. The shame you brought on me by doing this was nothing compared to the shame that you thought I would bring on your name by marrying.

Now, where my attempts at marrying are concerned there is much you can say in reply, and indeed you already have: you simply could not have much respect for my decision because I had twice broken off the engagement with F.* and twice reinstated it, after having needlessly dragged you and Mother to Berlin for the engagement, etc. That is all true, but how did it come about?

The fundamental idea behind both attempts at marrying was entirely respectable: to found a home, to gain independence. An idea with which you sympathize in theory, except that in practice it was just like that children's game where one child holds, even squeezes the other's hand, shouting as he grips: "Oh go away, go away, why don't you go?" This was certainly complicated in our case by the fact that your command for me to "go away" was always genuine, only unknown to you, the strength of your personality carried on holding me back, or rather holding me down.

Though both girls were chosen by chance, they were extraordinarily well chosen. It is further evidence of your complete misunderstanding that you can believe I, anxious, hesitant, suspicious, could choose a wife on a whim, carried away by the mere sight of a blouse. In truth both marriages would have been marriages of convenience, in as far as I had been completely preoccupied day and night, for years in the first case, months in the second, with their careful planning.

Neither of the girls disappointed me, only I disappointed them both. My opinion of them is exactly the same today as it was when I wanted to marry them.

Nor is it true that in my second attempt at marriage I ignored the experiences I had gained from the first, that I was reckless. The circumstances were so completely different, the things I had experienced in the first were the very things that gave me hope in the second, which was altogether much more promising. Here I do not want to go into details.

So why did I not marry? There were various individual obstacles as there are with everything, but life is about tackling such obstacles. The essential obstacle though, unfortunately quite independent from these particular events, was that I am clearly mentally incapable of marrying. That is evident from the fact that each time I resolve to marry, I cannot sleep, my head throbs day and night, life loses all meaning, I stagger about in despair. Anxiety is not the actual cause of this – though owing to my ponderous and pedantic nature I do suffer countless anxieties, but they have no real influence, like worms they apply the finishing touches to the corpse, but the decisive blow comes from elsewhere. We are dealing here with the general pressure of fear, of weakness, of self-contempt.

I want to try and explain more clearly: here in this attempt at marriage, two apparently conflicting forces in our relationship unite with greater force than anywhere else. Marriage certainly promises the clearest form of self-liberation and independence. Through it I would have a family, in my opinion the utmost that anyone can achieve, in this sense also the utmost that you achieved, I would be your equal, all the old and continuously self-renewing shame and tyranny would be consigned to history. That would certainly be wonderful, but also questionable. It is too much, it is impossible to achieve so much. It is as if a man were in prison, and intended not only to escape, which might be possible, but also and even simultaneously to convert the prison into his own pleasure dome. If he were to escape, he could not work on the conversion and if he were to stay and work on the conversion, he could not escape. If I want to gain independence in our own particular unfortunate relationship, I must do something which, as far as possible, has no connection with you at all; though marriage is the greatest thing of all and leads to the most honourable independence, it is at the same time intimately connected with you. To try to escape therefore has an element of madness about it, and every attempt to escape will almost certainly lead to madness.

Our close relationship is in part precisely what tempts me to marry. I picture the equality that it would bring about between the two of us, an equality that you would be able to understand like no other, an equality that would be so beautiful because it could make me a free, grateful, guiltless, upright son, you an untroubled, untyrannical, sympathetic, contented father. But in order to achieve this, everything that has ever happened would have to be undone, which means that we ourselves would have to be erased.

But as things currently stand between us, marriage is ruled out for me because it is your own exclusive domain. Sometimes I imagine a map of the earth laid out and you stretched diagonally across it. And then it seems to me that I can only lead my own life in those areas that are neither covered by your body, nor within your reach. And given the impression I have of your size, that leaves me with only a few, not very welcoming areas, and marriage in particular is not among them.

This very analogy proves that I am not at all trying to accuse you of hounding me out of marriage by your own example, as you hounded me out of the business. Quite the contrary, despite the remote similarities. Your marriage was in many respects a model marriage for me, a model of fidelity, mutual aid, number of children, and even when your children grew up to disturb the peace more and more, your marriage itself remained unshaken. Perhaps my high ideals of marriage were based on your example; but my desire to marry was doomed to failure for other reasons altogether. Notably your relationship with your children, which is indeed the theme of this whole letter.

It is thought by some that a fear of marrying sometimes originates in a fear that your children will one day take revenge on you for the sins that you committed against your own parents. This, I believe, has no great significance in my case, for my sense of guilt actually originates in you and is so imbued with its own uniqueness, indeed this sense of uniqueness is an integral part of its agonising nature, that any replication of it is unthinkable. Nonetheless, I must say that I would be unable to tolerate such a mute, tired, desiccated, ruined son as myself, as a last resort I would probably run away from him, emigrate, like you initially wanted to when you heard of my plans to marry. So perhaps this has after all influenced my incapacity to marry.

A much more important factor in this, however, is my anxiety about myself. This can be explained as follows: I have already implied that in my writing and everything connected with it, I have made little attempts at independence or escape, with the smallest imaginable success, they will scarcely lead anywhere, this has been confirmed many times for me. Despite this it is my duty, or rather my whole life's purpose to watch over these attempts, allow no danger, nor any potential danger to threaten them while I am capable of warding it off. Marriage represents just such a potential danger, admittedly also the greatest potential progress, but it is enough for me that it represents a potential danger. What lengths would I be driven to if it were a real danger? How could I live out a marriage in the perhaps undemonstrable but always undeniable sense of this danger? Faced with this possibility I may hesitate, but the final outcome is certain, I must renounce. Hence that old proverb is only very remotely applicable: that a bird in the hand is worth two in the bush. My hand is empty, the bush is full and yet – as dictated by the conditions of battle and the exigencies of life – I must choose emptiness. I had to make a similar choice when it came to my career.

The most significant obstacle to my marrying, though, is the no longer eradicable conviction that in order to keep a family together, let alone to guide it, I would need to have all the qualities I had observed in you, all rolled into one, good and bad, exactly as they are organically combined in you, your strength and yet your scorn of others, your health and yet a certain excess, your rhetorical skill and yet your inadequacy, your self-assurance and yet your dissatisfaction with everyone else, your worldly wisdom and yet your tyranny, your understanding of human nature and yet your mistrust of most people, then those merits of yours unfettered by weaknesses, such as your diligence, endurance, presence of mind and fearlessness. In comparison to you I possessed virtually none, or at least very few of these qualities, how could I dare to dream of marrying when I saw how even you struggled bitterly in your marriage, and how you still failed entirely where your children were concerned? Of course I never explicitly asked myself this question, nor did I answer it explicitly, otherwise my common sense would have intervened to overcome the problem and remind me of other men who are different to you (an example of one close by, and yet very different to you being Uncle Richard),* who have indeed married and have at least avoided crumbling under the pressure, which is in itself a worthy achievement and would have been more than enough for me. But I did not ask myself this question as such, rather I lived it out from my childhood onwards. My first test was not marriage, but rather various little trivialities; and in every little triviality you convinced me, through your example and through the way you brought me up, as I have tried to describe here, of my incapacity, and what was true of every triviality, proving you right in every case, had necessarily to be true of the most important thing of all – marriage. Until my attempts at marriage I grew up more or less like a businessman who lives from day to day having worries and nasty presentiments, but not keeping accurate accounts. He makes a few small profits which, due to their rarity, he always celebrates and exaggerates in his head, otherwise nothing but daily losses. Everything is recorded, but nothing balanced. Now comes the need to balance it all – that is to say, now comes marriage. And with the large sums that suddenly have to be dealt with, it is as if there had never even been the smallest profit, as if everything were one great debt. Marry now, without going mad!

This is how my life has been with you to date, and these are the prospects that my life holds for the future.

You might, when you read my explanation of why I am afraid of you, reply as follows: "You claim that I make it easier for myself simply by blaming you for the state of our relationship, but I believe that, despite apparent efforts, you make things not more difficult for yourself, but rather much more profitable. In the first instance you, like me, deny all guilt and responsibility, and so in this respect our behaviour is the same. But whereas I openly lay all the blame at your door, as I believe is correct, you choose to be both 'over-clever' and 'over-sensitive' and acquit me too of all guilt. You can, of course, only seem to succeed in the latter (you certainly wish for no more) and what emerges between the lines, in spite of all your 'clichés' about character and nature and antagonism and helplessness, is that I have been the true aggressor, while every action on your part was committed in self-defence. Even at this point you could be said, by your insincerity, to have achieved enough, for you have proved three things, firstly that you are innocent, secondly that I am guilty and thirdly that you are not only prepared to forgive me out of sheer magnanimity but, what is more and at the same time less, that you want to prove and believe for yourself, albeit in contradiction to the real truth, that I am also innocent. This ought to have been enough for you, but it is still not enough. You have got it into your head to claim that you live entirely off me. I admit that we battle with one another, but there are two sorts of battle.

That knightly battle in which independent opponents pit their strengths against each other, each fighting for himself, losing for himself, winning for himself. And then the battle fought by vermin, that not only bite but even go as far as to suck blood for the sake of preserving their own life. Professional soldiers do this, and so do you. You are incompetent when it comes to life; but in order to make things more comfortable, less stressful for you and to dispel your self-reproach, you seek to prove that I robbed you of your ability to cope and pocketed it for myself. Why should it bother you now that you are incompetent? It is after all my responsibility, now you only have to stretch yourself out and allow yourself to be dragged through life by me, both physically and mentally. An example: even while you expressed the desire to marry, you admit as much in this letter, you wanted at the same time not to marry, but, in order to save yourself from exertion, you wanted me to help you avoid marriage, by forbidding it on grounds that the union would bring 'shame' to my name. But that never occurred to me at all. Firstly, in this as in everything else, I never wanted to be an 'obstacle to your happiness', and secondly I would never want to hear this sort of reproach from a child of mine. But did the self-restraint that I exercised in leaving you free to marry do me any good? Not in the slightest. An aversion to the marriage on my part would not have prevented it from taking place, on the contrary, it would in itself have been another incentive for you to marry the girl, for it would have meant the successful completion of your 'attempt at escaping', as you put it. And my consent to your marriage did not prevent you from reproaching me, for you prove that I am in any case to blame for your failure to marry. Fundamentally though, in this as in everything else, you have only proved to me that all my reproaches have been justified, and that one especially justified reproach was still lacking, namely reproach of your insincerity, your fawning, your feeding off me. If I am not sorely mistaken, you are feeding off me even with this letter."

To this I reply firstly that this whole reproach, which can in part be turned back against you, comes not from you but rather from me. Not even your mistrust of others is as great as my own self-mistrust, instilled in me by you. I do not deny that there is some justification for this reproach, which in itself contributes new material to the explanation of our relationship. In reality, of course, things cannot fit together as neatly as the evidence in my letter, life is more complicated than a jigsaw puzzle; but with the adjustment that this reproach brings, an adjustment on which I am neither able nor willing to elaborate, I have reached something that in my opinion so closely resembles the truth, that it might comfort us both a little and make it easier for us to live and die.

Franz

Extracts from Kafka's Diaries

1911

26th August. Tomorrow I am supposed to travel to Italy. This evening Father could not sleep for excitement and sheer anxiety about his business, which has made him ill. A damp cloth on his chest, nausea, difficulty in breathing, pacing up and down, sighing. Mother is fearful, but finds new consolation in the fact that he has always been so energetic, he has always coped with everything, and now – I tell her the trouble with the business cannot last more than another three months, and that everything will then be fine. He paces up and down, sighing and shaking his head. He is aware that we cannot take on his burden or otherwise rid him of it, but even we are aware, despite our good intentions, of the sad necessity that he must provide for his family… Through his frequent yawning or his (incidentally not revolting) nose-picking, Father reassures us slightly, barely perceptibly, about his condition – even though he generally never does this when healthy.

31st October. …In case my father should ever again call me a bad son, I am writing down now, so as not to forget, that

he, in front of several relatives and without particular reason
– perhaps simply to make me feel small or perhaps because
he means to save me – called Max a *"meshuggener ritoch"*,*
and that yesterday, when Löwy was in my room, he spoke
with ironic bodily convulsions and contortions of the mouth
of all the strangers that are being allowed into the flat, asking
what one could possibly find of interest in strangers, or why
one should ever enter into such useless relationships, etc…
But I should not have written this down, as I have positively
written myself into a state of hatred for my father, a hatred
for which he has given me no cause today, a hatred which,
at least as far as his statements about Löwy are concerned, is
disproportionately great, and a hatred which is increased by
the fact that I cannot actually remember anything vicious in
the way Father behaved yesterday.

16th October. Exhausting Sunday yesterday. The entire staff
handed Father its resignation. Through kind words and
congeniality, and exploiting his illness, his great presence and
previous vigour, his experience and cleverness, he won them
back, almost all of them, in general and private discussions.

3rd November. …Löwy – my father's view: "He who sleeps
with dogs wakes up with fleas." I could not contain myself
and said something out of order. Whereupon Father replied,

particularly calmly (admittedly considerably later, after we had discussed other things): "You know that I am not to be worked up and must be treated carefully. So don't come to me with these things now. I have had just about enough excitement, more than enough. So spare me such talk." I say: "I am doing my utmost to hold back," and sense in Father, as always in such intense moments, an underlying wisdom of which I can only catch the slightest pulse.

5th November. ...I want to write, my head is throbbing. I sit in my room, surrounded by the clamour of the entire flat. I hear all the doors slamming, at least their racket spares me the footsteps going between them, but I can still hear the oven door banging shut in the kitchen. Father bursts into my room and out the other side, his dressing gown trailing behind him, in the next room I can hear ash being scraped out of the stove, Valli asks into the unknown, through the anteroom, as if across a Parisian alleyway, whether Father's hat has been polished yet, this well-intentioned whisper provokes a scream in reply. The front door is unlatched, creaking like a catarrhal throat, then opened further with the brief sound of a woman singing, then shut with a dull masculine jolt, a most inconsiderate sound. Father is gone, now begins the more tender, more diffuse, more hopeless din of the canaries. Much earlier I had considered, but am now reminded again by the canaries, whether to open the door a little, creep snake-like into the next room and, lying on the floor, ask my sisters and their nanny to be quiet.

14th December. This morning my father reproached me for not caring about the factory. I explained that I had bought shares expecting to profit, but I couldn't contribute to the work as long as I was in the office. Father continued arguing, I stood by the window and remained silent. But that evening I found myself thinking, as a result of our morning discussion, that I could declare myself very satisfied with my current position and must only be wary of having all my time free for literature.

26th December. …It is unpleasant to listen to Father when he – with endless digressions on the fortunate situation of contemporaries and, above all, his children – recounts the sufferings that he had to endure in his youth. Nobody denies that for years he had open sores on his legs, as a consequence of insufficient winter clothing; that he frequently went hungry; that at the tender age of ten, he had to push a cart from village to village, even in winter and very early in the morning – but these true facts, even combined with the further true fact that I haven't been through all this myself, do not in the slightest warrant his conclusion that I have been happier than him, that the sores on his legs somehow make him superior to me, nor the assumption he has always made that I cannot do justice to his former life and finally, that I, precisely because I have not experienced the same sufferings, should be infinitely grateful. How happy I would be to hear him speak uninterruptedly of his youth and his parents, but it torments me to listen to it spoken in such a boastful and antagonistic tone. Time and again he claps his hands together, saying: "Who appreciates that these days? What do these children know? Nobody's been through what I have! Can any child understand that today?"

1912

7th January. ...The noise of card-playing could be heard in the large room, and later the loud, albeit incoherent conversation which Father usually has when he is feeling well, as he is today – a conversation that I could only hear spasmodically above the background noise. Little Felix was sleeping in the girls' room, with the door wide open. I slept on the other side, in my room. The door to my room was closed, out of consideration for my age. The open door further demonstrated that they still intended to lure Felix into the family, while I had already been shut out.

6th May. ...A recent dream:

I was travelling with my father through Berlin by tram. Countless turnpikes, standing upright at regular intervals, painted in two colours and rounded to a blunt point, contributed to the urban feel. Apart from that the city was virtually empty, but the concentration of these turnpikes was considerable. We came to a gate, alighted without being aware of it, went through the gate. Behind the gate was a very steep wall, which my father climbed as if dancing, his legs flying, it was so easy for him. There was a certain lack of consideration in the way he did not help me, as I could only ascend with the utmost effort, on all fours, frequently sliding back again, as if the wall below me had become steeper. It also embarrassed me that the [wall] was soiled with human excrement, so that flakes of it clung to me, mostly on my chest.

I looked down at the filth and ran my hand over it. When I finally reached the top, my father, who was already emerging from a building, immediately threw his arms around my neck, and hugged and kissed me. He was wearing an old-fashioned, short frock-coat padded like a sofa on the inside, which was very familiar to me from past memory. "This Dr von Leyden! What an outstanding man," he kept exclaiming. But he had not visited him in his capacity as a doctor, merely as a man worth knowing. I was slightly scared that I would have to go inside and meet him, but this was not required. Behind to the left, I saw a man with his back to me, sitting in a room consisting entirely of glass walls. It turned out that this man was the Professor's secretary, that my father had in fact spoken only with him and not the Professor himself, but that he had somehow seen the merits of the Professor embodied in the secretary, thus entitling him to form a full judgment of the Professor, as if he had spoken with him personally.

1914

6th May. My parents seem to have found a nice flat for F. and me; I wandered around aimlessly for an entire afternoon. Will they also lower me into my grave, after a life made happy through their care?

19th December. ...Yesterday Father reproached me about the factory: "You've dropped me right in it." I then went home and wrote calmly for three hours, aware of the fact that my guilt, although undeniable, is not as great as Father claims. Today, Saturday, I did not go to supper, partly for fear of Father, partly to make full use of the night for work, but I wrote only one page, and not a very good one at that.

1916

19th April. ...I dreamt recently: We were living on the Graben near the Café Continental. A regiment was coming round the corner of the Herrengasse, heading for the Staatsbahnhof. My father says: "Something like this has to be seen while one is capable of it," and swings himself (in Felix's brown nightgown, his figure becoming an amalgamation of both) up onto the window and, with outstretched arms, splays his legs out on the very wide, steeply slanting window ledge. I grab him and hold on to him by the two small loops meant for the cord of his nightgown. To be perverse he stretches out even further, it takes all my strength to hold him. I think of how good it would be if I could rope my feet to some fixed object, so as not to be pulled down with Father. This, however, would require letting go of Father, at least momentarily, which I cannot do. Sleep – especially my sleep – cannot survive all this stress, and I wake up.

18th October. ...I am descended from my parents, bound to them and my sisters by blood, I do not feel it in my everyday life or, as a consequence of this inevitable obsession, in my specific plans, but deep down I am more aware of it than I know. Sometimes it moves me to hatred, a glimpse of the parental bed at home, the dirty bedclothes, the carefully laid-out shirts can make me vomit, can turn me inside out, it's as if I wasn't fully born yet, as if I repeatedly came into the world afresh, from this dull life in this dull living room, as if I must seek to validate myself there over and over again, as if I were indissolubly bound to these repulsive things, in part if not wholly, the bond is still attached to my feet, preventing them from walking, from escaping the original formless mush. That is how it is sometimes.

But at other times I remember that they are my parents after all, necessary sources of strength and elements of my own being, belonging to me not only as an obstacle but also as a part of myself. Then I want them as one wants all the best things: if I, in all my malice, vulgarity, selfishness and lovelessness, have always shuddered at the thought of them and indeed still do so today, because one cannot break these habits, and if they – Father from one side, Mother from the other – have, again out of necessity, almost broken my will, then I want at least to think them worthy of this. I have been betrayed by them, but I cannot defy the laws of nature without going mad – hence more hatred and nothing but hatred.

1917

21st September. ...A dream about Father: In front of a small audience (Frau Fanta was there, to give you an idea),

Father talks publicly for the first time about an idea for social reform. Father wants this select audience – especially select in his opinion – to devise the propaganda for this idea. On the surface Father's language is much more modest, in that he only asks the party, once they know all the details, to supply him with the addresses of people interested in the idea, who could then be invited to a large public assembly in the near future. My father has never had anything to do with any of these people before, this leads him to take them excessively seriously, to put on a black suit jacket and present the idea with extreme precision, with all the hallmarks of a dilettante. Those present realize from the start, although they were not prepared for this speech, that this is merely an old, worn-out idea from long ago, presented with all the pride of originality. They let Father feel this. But the latter was ready for this objection, so, with splendid confidence that the objection is without substance, although it seems to have tempted even him several times, he presents his case even more emphatically, with a subtle bitter smile. Once he has finished, it is apparent from the generally disgruntled murmur that he has failed to persuade them of the originality and practicality of his idea. Not many of them will be interested in it. In spite of this he finds the occasional person who, because of his good nature or perhaps because he is acquainted with me, supplies him with some addresses. My father, wholly unperturbed by the general atmosphere, has put away his lecture notes and taken out some small piles of pre-prepared white slips to note down the addresses. I can only hear the name of a Court Counsellor Strýzǎnowski, or something similar.

Later I see Father sitting on the floor and leaning against the sofa, his usual position when he plays with Felix. Startled, I ask him what he's doing. He's thinking about his idea.

1921

25th October. ...My parents were playing cards; I sat with them on my own, a complete stranger; Father said I should join in or at least watch; I somehow found an excuse not to. What did this refusal, an act I had repeated many times since childhood, signify? This invitation offered me the chance to live a social, even to a certain extent public life, by joining in I would have been able to fulfil their expectations, not well but tolerably, playing would not even have bored me that much – yet I declined. In light of that, I am wrong to complain that I was never swept up in the current of life, that I never got away from Prague, was never exposed to any sport or trade, and so on – I would probably always have declined the offers, just as I had the invitation to play. Only pointless things got through to me, the law degree, the office, then later further pointless things, such as gardening, carpentry and the like, in doing these things I behaved like someone who throws a needy beggar out and then plays the role of benefactor in private, giving alms from his right hand to his left.

But I always declined, probably out of general weakness, and in particular weakness of will, I only came to understand this relatively late. I used to interpret this tendency to decline as a good sign (seduced by the generally great hopes I had for myself), today only a vestige of this generous interpretation survives.

2nd December. Writing letters in my parents' room. The signs of decline are unimaginable. Recently the belief that I was defeated by Father as a small boy and have since been prevented by pride from leaving the battleground, throughout all these years, despite enduring defeat over and over again.

Extracts from Kafka's Letters

I almost never quarrel with my parents, who are now in good health and good spirits. My father gets annoyed with me only when he sees me sitting at my desk too late, because he thinks I am working too hard. My health is better than it has been for a few months, at least it was at the beginning of the week... Life at home has been almost entirely peaceful.

to Max Brod, 1910

What I am doing is simple and self evident: in the city, in my family, in my profession, in society, in love (you can put this first if you like), in my relations to the community as it stands or as I would wish it to be, in all these I have failed, and moreover – I have observed this clearly – in a way that no one else around me has. It is that fundamental childlike idea: "No one is as bad as me", which later, when corrected, only causes new pain. But here we are no longer dealing with badness and self-reproach, rather with the patent psychological fact of failing – nonetheless this idea persists and will persist. I don't want to boast of a suffering that I have never experienced, my suffering seems in retrospect (as it has always seemed at every little stage along the way) all too undeservedly slight compared to the pressure it has had to withstand – nonetheless it was too great to be borne much longer, or if it was not too great, it was too meaningless. (In this murk, it is perhaps understandable to look for meaning.) The most immediate escape, perhaps from childhood onwards, was not suicide, but the thought of it. In my case I was prevented from committing suicide not by any cowardice, but merely the thought, which likewise ended in meaninglessness: "You, who are incapable of doing anything, you think you can do this? How dare you think that? If you were capable of killing yourself, you wouldn't really have to any more." Etc. Later, as I slowly gained more insight, I stopped thinking of suicide.

to Max Brod, 1917

…may I ask you at any rate to arrange the stories in the order I specified. May I further ask you to insert a dedication page with the inscription "To My Father".

to Kurt Wolff Verlag, his publisher, 1918

Ever since I decided to dedicate the book to my father, I am anxious for it to appear soon. Not that this would appease my father; our antagonism is too deeply rooted, but at least I would have done something; although unable to emigrate to Palestine, I would at least have traced the route on the map.

to Max Brod, 1918

When I was younger, whenever I committed some apparent stupidity which actually stemmed from a fundamental flaw in my nature, my father used to say, "Just like Rudolph!" comparing me to an utterly ridiculous stepbrother of my mother's, an indecipherable, over-friendly, over-modest, solitary and yet almost garrulous man. Fundamentally I had hardly anything in common with him, my critical father aside. But the painful repetition of the comparison, the almost physical difficulty of avoiding at all costs a route I had not even intended to take, and finally my father's persuasiveness, or if you like, the curse he put on me, made me start at least to resemble this uncle.

to Robert Klopstock, 1921

...I might have stayed if I had seen that my father needed me in any way. But yesterday that was not the case at all. His affection for me dwindled day by day (no, on the second day it was at its greatest, but after that it diminished constantly). And yesterday he could not get me out of the room quickly enough, although he compelled my mother to stay. A new, especially wearing period of suffering now begins for my mother, even if everything carries on as well as it did before. For while until now my father, gripped by terrible memories, has considered staying in bed a blessing, he now finds that lying still has become a torture (he has a scar on his back, which has always made it virtually impossible for him to lie still for long periods; in addition, each change of position is difficult for his heavy body, then there is his irregular heart, the bulky bandage, the renewed pain when he coughs, but above all his restless, helpless and benighted mind; the way I see it, he now faces a torture greater than any he has faced before; this torture has become apparent since his condition improved, yesterday he gestured with his hand behind the nurse, whom I find wonderful, as she left, a gesture that in his language could only mean "Bitch!" And this state of his (which perhaps only I can grasp in all its bare awfulness) will go on for another ten days at the very least, and whatever of it can be taken out on my mother will be taken out on her to its full extent. Ten such day-and-night vigils now await my poor mother!

to Max Brod, 20th July 1922

What Herr Weltsch reports is hardly compelling, he takes it for granted that all fathers love and praise their sons. But in my case what reason could there be for my father's eyes to light up? A son incapable of marriage, unable to pass on the family name; pensioned off at thirty-nine; occupied with nothing but his weird writing, which deals only with his salvation or damnation; loveless; unbelieving, unable even to pray for salvation; tuberculosis-stricken, and as his father quite properly sees it, having brought the sickness upon himself, since no sooner was he released from the nursery for a moment, than he sought out that unhealthy room at the Schönborn Palace, despite his total incapacity for independence. A son to rave about.

to Max Brod, late July 1922

Note on the Texts

The translations have been based on the following German texts: *'Brief an den Vater'* in *Nachgelassene Schriften und Fragmente II* (Frankfurt am M.: S. Fischer, 1992–93), *Gesammelte Werke*, ed. Max Brod (Frankfurt am M: S. Fischer, 1953) and *Tagebücher 1910–1923* ed. Max Brod (Frankfurt am M.: S. Fischer, 1951).

Notes

p. 7, *Und verstehe... Advokatenbrief*: Kafka, *Briefe an Milena* (Frankfurt am M.: S. Fischer, 1952), p. 80.

p. 7, *Du... zu haben*: Kafka, *'Brief an den Vater'* in *Nachgelassene Schriften und Fragmente II* (Frankfurt am M.: S. Fischer, 1992–93), p. 152.

p. 8, *Du wirktest... musstest*: Ibid., p. 147.

p. 8, *Upbringing... marriage*: Anz, Thomas, 'Afterword' in Reppin, Karen, *Letter to the Father* (Prague: Vitalis, 1998), p. 84.

p. 9, *neglecting... son*: Robertson suggests that it was typical for Jews of Hermann Kafka's generation to neglect their religious traditions as they tried to integrate into non-Jewish society in Prague: Robertson, Ritchie, *Franz Kafka: Judaism, Politics and Literature* (Oxford: Clarendon, 1987), p. 5.

p. 9, *anxiety... sexuality*: Anz, Thomas, 'Afterword' in Reppin, Karen, *Letter to the Father* (Prague: Vitalis, 1998), p. 84.

p. 10, *Brod published... stories*: *Brief an den Vater* was originally published in *'Hochzeitsvorbereitungen auf dem Lande und andere Prosa aus dem Nachlass'* in *Gesammelte Werke*, ed. Max Brod (Frankfurt am M.: S. Fischer, 1953).

p. 11, *Ich... weg*: Kafka, *Das Urteil* (Frankfurt am M.: S. Fischer, 1974), p. 17.

p. 11, *weil... Gans*: Ibid., p. 15.

p. 11, *Sie hat... verstehn*: Kafka, *'Brief an den Vater'* in *Nachgelassene Schriften und Fragmente II* (Frankfurt am M.: S. Fischer, 1992–93), p. 205.

p. 11, *Georg... Kafka*: Kafka, *Tagebücher 1910–23*, ed. Max Brod (Frankfurt am M.: S. Fischer, 1951), p. 297.

p. 12, *an identity... Anz*: Anz, Thomas, 'Afterword' in Reppin, Karen, *Letter to the Father* (Prague: Vitalis, 1998), pp. 84–87.

p. 18, *Franzensbad*: A spa town in the Czech Republic.

p. 18, *Ottla's*: The youngest of Kafka's three sisters.

p. 19, *Robert Kafka... Karl Hermann*: Robert Kafka was Franz Kafka's cousin, with an admirable physique and successful career. Karl Hermann was Franz's equally successful brother-in-law (married to Franz's eldest sister, Elli). Hermann Kafka made no secret of his opinion that Franz was inferior to these relatives.

p. 20, *Löwy*: Löwy was the maiden name of Franz's mother, Julie Kafka.

p. 20, *Uncles Philipp, Ludwig and Heinrich*: Three of Hermann Kafka's brothers.

p. 21, *Valli*: The second eldest of Franz's three sisters.

p. 22, *pavlatche*: A balcony running along the edge of a house on the first floor or above, inside the exterior wall (Czech).

p. 24, *Pepa*: Ottla's husband (Josef David).

p. 25, *meshugge*: "Mad" (Yiddish slang).

p. 27, *Löwy*: A friend through whom Franz made his first acquaintance with the Yiddish theatre. Franz's diary entries show that he felt a rare spiritual connection with Löwy.

p. 27, *proverb... dogs and fleas*: A western proverb: "He who sleeps with dogs wakes up with fleas".

p. 30, *Felix's*: The son of Elli Kafka and Karl Hermann; Hermann Kafka's grandson.

p. 31, *her*: The "she" to which Hermann Kafka refers is never explicitly identified.

p. 41, *Pisek*: A town situated 100 km south of Prague near Hermann's home town of Wossek.

p. 44, *Assicurazioni Generali*: Italian insurance firm where Kafka spent an unhappy year (1907–08). The schedule prevented him from writing, he termed the job a "*Brotberuf*" (one done solely for the sake of earning a living).

p. 50, *Karl*: Karl Hermann, see note to p. 19.

p. 50, *Gerti*: Gerti Wasner, with whom Franz had a ten-day love affair in 1913.

p. 52, *Irma*: One of Hermann's nieces (Ludwig's daughter).

p. 58, *Seder*: The Passover Seder, a symbolic feast held at home on the first and second evenings of Passover.

p. 58, *High Holy Days*: A sacred period observed during the first ten days of Tishri (the seventh month of the Jewish calendar), between Rosh Hashanah and Yom Kippur.

p. 61, *Franklin's*: Benjamin Franklin, whose autobiography partly inspired Kafka's novel *Amerika*.

p. 65, *Schönborn Palace*: A building, now the United States Embassy in the Mala Strana district of Prague.

p. 72, *Josefsplatz*: A piazza near the Kafkas' home in Prague.

p. 76, *F.*: Felice Bauer, twice engaged to Franz. The pair met in 1912 and maintained an intensive correspondence until Franz was diagnosed with tuberculosis in 1917 and the affair ended.

p. 83, *Uncle Richard*: One of Franz's uncles on his mother's side.

p. 90, *meshuggener ritoch*: "Hot-headed madman" (Yiddish slang).

Acknowledgements

The publisher would like to thank William Chamberlain and Alexander Feest for their care in the editing of this work.

ONEWORLD CLASSICS

ONEWORLD CLASSICS aims to publish mainstream and lesser-known European classics in an innovative and striking way, while employing the highest editorial and production standards. By way of a unique approach the range offers much more, both visually and textually, than readers have come to expect from contemporary classics publishing.

∽

CHARLOTTE BRONTË: *Jane Eyre*

EMILY BRONTË: *Wuthering Heights*

ANTON CHEKHOV: *Sakhalin Island*
Translated by Brian Reeve

ANTON CHEKHOV: *The Woman in the Case*
Translated by Kyril FitzLyon

CHARLES DICKENS: *Great Expectations*

CHARLES DICKENS: *The Haunted House*

D.H. LAWRENCE: *The First Women in Love*

D.H. LAWRENCE: *The Second Lady Chatterley's Lover*

D.H. LAWRENCE: *The Fox*

D.H. LAWRENCE: *Paul Morel*

D.H. LAWRENCE: *Selected Letters*

JAMES HANLEY: *Boy*

JAMES HANLEY: *The Closed Harbour*

JACK KEROUAC: *Beat Generation*

JANE AUSTEN: *Emma*

JANE AUSTEN: *Pride and Prejudice*

JANE AUSTEN: *Sense and Sensibility*

JANE AUSTEN: *Persuasion*

JANE AUSTEN: *Love and Friendship*

WILKIE COLLINS: *The Moonstone*

GIUSEPPE GIOACCHINO BELLI: *Sonnets*
Translated by Mike Stocks

DANIEL DEFOE: *Robinson Crusoe*

ROBERT LOUIS STEVENSON: *Treasure Island*

GIACOMO LEOPARDI: *Canti*
Translated by J.G. Nichols

OSCAR WILDE: *The Picture of Dorian Gray*

OSCAR WILDE: *The Decay of Lying*

GEOFFREY CHAUCER: *Canterbury Tales*
Adapted into modern English by Chris Lauer